MW00903828

POST OFFICE

Tim Reaume

Copyright 2012 Tim Reaume

ISBN-13: 978-1500104955
ISBN-10: 1500104957

TITLE Revised November 2013
Formerly "POSTAL"

Discover other titles by Tim Reaume:

The Jade Jaguar

Reclaiming The Void

www.timreaume.com

Dedications:

To my beautiful wife, Gayle, to our amazing and beautiful children, and to my dear, sweet mom. This book is also dedicated to the hardworking, steadfast men and woman of the postal service, from conscientious management to under-appreciated labor.

Chapter 1

"In a democracy, civil disobedience and moral rebellion are partners in freedom. Ain't that right, Brian?" He stopped his pacing in front of the luncheon table in the swing room to stare down at Brian.

"You read too much, Tom." Jessica unwrapped a tuna fish sandwich and hesitated before she bit into it. "Remember, Tom," she said slowly, as if speaking to a child, "A mind is a terrible thing to waste. A couple of brain cells should only be asked to absorb so much information in such a short time."

"Arrgh!" was the typical response that Brian had come to expect from Tom, and when he watched a satisfied Jessica bite into her sandwich, he had to grin.

"I'm serious, Brian." Tom sounded hurt.

"I'm not really into politics," he said. Tom looked like a sad but giant six-foot eight-inch, three hundred pound teddy bear.

"What are you into, Brian?" Jessica asked keeping a steady eye on him. She slowly licked a piece of tuna fish from her upper lip.

Brian twisted uncomfortably in his chair.

"But if you just accept everything you are told, you are no longer free—the people who interpret the rules in self-serving ways gain total control. Pretty soon you'd be serving them, and your democracy is shot to shit."

"You're taking this pretty seriously, aren't you?" asked Brian.

"Yes!" Ramon and Jimmy walked into the swing room and sat down. Tom pointed and said, "Ask Jimmy what happens to people who don't fight oppression and domination at its roots."

"OK," said Jimmy. "I'll tell ya, bro. Those poor Northern Irish live under a dark fucking cloud."

Tom looked puzzled for a moment. "No, I mean like you, Jimmy. Blacks."

Jimmy looked shocked. "Black? Like me? I's black? Oh, Lawdy, Lawdy!"

"Arrgh!" said Tom as he stood, shaking his head. "For Christ's sake, what are you all—slaves to your own ignorance?"

"I'm just a dancin' fool, bro. Dip and duck from the punches. Run and hide 'til the trouble finds you."

"You can't keep on running, though," he said to Jimmy, pleading with him. "That's my point. Nothing ever changes until you turn around and fight. People have even died for their causes."

"Did you by any chance get another letter of warning, Tom?" Brian asked as Tom started out of the room.

"Yes, goddamn it!"

"He was an hour late for work Monday morning," Jessica said. She rolled her eyes. "He lives a mile away from work, but he got 'stuck in traffic.' Can you believe it?"

Tom put a big meaty hand on the door and leaned back in. "My home is in Mexico. Enjoy your slavery."

With that he turned and went out on the dock to sort raw mail.

"Mexico?" asked Jessica.

"He speaks better Spanish than I do," said Ramon. "I've heard he was raised by some Mexican-Indians. He has a house here but still thinks of his old village in Mexico as home."

If Ramon had heard that, they all knew it was true. Ramon knew a little something about everyone.

"Seems like we don't know as much about Tom as we thought we did," said Jessica.

"We know the sucker's leading the league in L.O.W.'s," said Jimmy.

"If he gets another letter of warning he'll be suspended again," said Ramon.

"Maybe he's right," said Brian. He shook his head and began scooping up his lunch bag and sandwich wrappers. "Whipcracker and Dunn have been dumping all over us lately."

"And don't forget that mutha-fuckin' Weasel," Jimmy added vehemently.

"Wish we had a postmaster with balls," said Jessica.

Brian laughed. "I didn't know we had a postmaster at all."

"If he had any balls, we wouldn't have half the problems we do."

"What's he look like?" Brian asked Jimmy.

"Henry Whynaught? Sucker's about $6,000 dollars lighter than he used to be for stickin' up for that slimeball, Weasel." Jimmy's smile reflected his personal satisfaction. He was referring to an EEO case he had won against the Post Office. Tom had his way of beating the system, or equaling the odds, as Jimmy would rather put it, and he had his.

Brian stood up and was immediately embarrassed by Jessica's bold once over.

"Oo-wee! That Karen better appreciate what she's got, honey."

Brian made his escape to the reg-cage trying to ignore the burning in his cheeks. Her flirting would be much easier to accept if she weren't so beautiful and so single-minded in her advances. The longer he stayed around her, the more he felt his defenses melting. She was obvious in her intentions, and Brian found that to be quite a weapon against his resolve.

But he always found refuge in the reg-cage.

The reg-cage really was a cage—it was a ten foot square, wire-walled and wire-ceilinged container in the middle of the workroom floor, standing ten feet high. Brian dug out his key and entered. Moments after signing in he was on a rolling stool near the back of the cage writing up second notices on some of the C.O.D.s stacked on the floor.

Lenny Nicks walked up and stuck his head into the pass-through opening where Brian transferred accountables to the carriers. Lenny was standing up on his toes, once again trying to compensate for his short stature in any way he could. Sometimes he stood on his toes; sometimes he stepped on the toes of others. Either way bumped him up to imagined heights he could never reach based on personality or respect alone.

"McGraw! I got a late carrier." He frowned as Brian looked up. "I need him on the street, now!"

Brian stood up from his second notices and walked over. "No problem, Nicks."

Lenny scowled at the emphasis Brian painted on "Nicks," and he said, "Are you trying to be funny?"

Brian sighed and stared at him.

"Just give him his crap so I can get his ass in the street. Now!" He slammed a finger down on the ledge to accentuate his demand, staring for a moment at Brian.

Brian shrugged.

"Soon as you move."

Lenny's face reddened, and after a final glare he whipped around and stalked away. Lou Lambier casually leaned onto the reg-window ledge, and he and Brian followed the Weasel's departure, the hitch in Weasel's step giving away his fresh irritation at another disrespectful employee blind to the royal treatment he deserved.

"I got into a little trouble for being late this morning." Lou was still frowning after Lenny's fleeing figure. "I think I might have pissed him off, but I can't be sure. He's always like that."

"Still want to be a supervisor?" Brian asked him.

Lou turned and grinned. He occasionally substituted for one of the regular supervisors, and was seriously considering it. "If I do, I think I'll have some big shoes to fill."

"Gigantic." They both laughed, not at any of the Weasel's shortcomings, but at the importance of superiority the Weasel put on himself in compensating for his own perceived deficiencies. No one cared but Lenny, but his constant hostile demeanor made his insecurities open targets for those he tried to bully.

Brian issued two registers and ten certified letters to Lou, and Lou signed for them. As the register clerk Brian controlled all of the valuable articles of mail, or accountables, such as C.O.D.'s, registered mail, and certified mail that needed to be signed for by carriers before they took them to the street to hand deliver to customers.

People who sent out mail in this secure manner wanted a paper trail of delivery. Lou would now get signatures as he delivered each letter, or he would leave a notice to show the customer that the Bay City Post Office now had it, ready for them to pick up at their convenience. A second notice would be sent out a few days later if still unclaimed. If not picked up at all, at the end of the notification period it would be returned to the sender.

"Got a couple of Princess House C.O.D.'s for you, too," Brian said. He opened the cage door to slide the two large parcels out to Lou. C.O.D.'s, or collect-on-delivery items, were a little different than other accountables—they required payment as well as a signature before they could be delivered.

Breaking the accountable chain by losing either the article or proof of delivery could jeopardize a postal career, and in a city the size of Bay City, the accountables stacked up. Working the reg-cage kept Brian busy and on his toes.

Lou grabbed the nearby dolly and piled the C.O.D.'s on top of each other to take to his vehicle.

"Try to stay out of trouble," Brian said with a nod toward Weasel's duty desk.

"No problem. At least I get to go out on the street." Brian shook his head and frowned, and Lou grinned, adding, "You're the one who has to stay in here all day with those clowns."

"No reprieve," Brian agreed. Lou hurried down the aisle toward the loading dock, and Brian repeated softly, "No frickin' reprieve."

At noon he was working on writing up C.O.D. second notices near the back of the cage when he heard Tom and Whipcracker arguing next to the time clock fifteen feet away.

"How could you lose my leave request?" Tom asked.

Whipcracker looked up defiantly at Tom and asked, "What request?"

Brian groaned at the all too familiar confrontation.

"You keep telling me I have to wait two days for approval, then you lose the damn thing."

"I don't know what you're talking about, Short. If you want Thursday and Friday off this week, I think it's a little late to be submitting a leave request." He grinned malevolently while scratching his rotund belly and added, "If you want to submit for next week, however, there's still time."

"Aw fuck!" said Tom slamming the time clock and replacing his card. "You'd just conveniently lose that mother-fucker, too."

"Hey; if you need to discuss this problem of yours..." Whipcracker was positively beaming.

Tom stared balefully, just long enough to break down Whipcracker's surge of gratification, and then he turned on his heels and stomped toward the dock exit.

Brian went up to collect registers from the customer window.

Teeth was flirting with a young woman while he weighed her package. He was a part-time flexible clerk filling in for Bob Higgins who had recently retired. Teeth had put in for a supervisory job in Spring Valley and talked as if he were sure to get it. He was forty-four years old and had spent twenty years in the post office, most of it back east from where he had transferred six months ago. He hadn't put enough time into the Bay City office yet to become a regular clerk, but his knowledge of the window had him filling in for the retired Higgins. Brian liked him and had decided he'd make a good supervisor—that was the only thing he had going against him as far as the appointment to Spring Valley went. But then again, maybe Spring Valley appreciated good supervisors.

"Hey, Brian. I was telling her that she gets the special rate. What do you think—does she qualify?"

The young woman with the baby in her arms was enjoying the attention, and Brian looked at her.

"Oh, yeah," he said. "Easily."

Brian grinned when Teeth smiled his big ivory smile and told her, "For you, only two seventy-four." That was the normal rate and the woman knew it. It seemed to Brian that to be successful on the window, a clerk had to have an incredibly easy going personality. He'd miss Teeth when he was gone to Spring Valley.

Brian picked up the registers and signed delivery notices and went back to the cage. He wondered who would be taking the place Teeth was subbing for. So far management hadn't posted Bob Higgins vacated job and no one had been given an opportunity to bid on it. They seemed to have something planned out for the position already, but these managers acted as if the information was a government secret.

I hope Teeth doesn't take his cue from what he's seen here, Brian thought. Tom Short had recently submitted for three leave requests that Brian knew of, and each of them had somehow been misplaced or lost by his and everybody else's good buddy Whipcracker. But that was only the tip of the iceberg. Between Whipcracker, Phyllis Dunn, Darrell Diamond and Lenny Nicks, who had earned the nickname Weasel, a kind of dark cloud had been slowly settling down upon the employees of the Bay City Post Office. And Postmaster Henry Whynaught had done little to relieve the atmosphere with his invisible act.

*****

Brian felt the cold when he rode his Suzuki home that evening. The early bite of winter—still three months away—was in the air, and although mild in southern California, it was still more evident on a motorcycle.

Karen was home, for a change, and thankfully delivered pizza was to be the main course. Charlie and Natalie Sharp were sitting in the living room when he walked in.

"It's Friday!" he said. He noticed Karen reaching into the refrigerator and a look of panic crossed his face. "Who let her into the kitchen?" Despite her occasional valiant efforts, Karen and the kitchen were a volatile combination.

"No sweat," said Charlie swinging his lanky body around to grin at her. "She's just grabbing me a beer."

"Oh, ease up, you guys," Natalie said. "Don't you think you're a little hard on her?" She had her legs crossed and an arm over the back of the couch. She looked comfortable in her blue jeans and yellow sweatshirt sitting next to Charlie.

"Yeah," said Brian sarcastically while tossing his gloves and helmet into the entryway closet. "Tuesday she burned a perfectly good Caesar's salad." He looked up hopefully. "We're still having pizza, aren't we?"

"Why do you pick on her?" asked Natalie.

"Natalie would like something to eat, Karen," Charlie said with a grin.

"No, thank you," said Natalie quickly. "Go ahead—pick on her."

"OK, you wise guys," said Karen. She let the refrigerator door shut and pulled a bottle opener from a drawer. "I've been working hard, too. And unlike you weekday warriors, I will also be working hard tomorrow. I really don't need this abuse."

She settled onto the couch on the other side of Charlie and handed him a Corona.

"I should be happy," Brian said while walking over to plop into an easy chair. "At least you're home tonight."

When Karen frowned and took a deep breath Charlie and Natalie exchanged a quick glance.

"So, you'd rather I stayed home, had babies and spent hours in the kitchen cooking up meals for you?" She stared at Brian, adding, "I could save a lot on shoes, too, running around barefoot and all."

"Everyone can't be like my little Natalie," said Charlie, trying to break the tension. Natalie looked at him in disbelief, and then punched him in the arm.

"C'mon, honey," said Brian. "I'm only kidding—in a selfish way."

"I know." She slumped forward and picked up her bottle of beer, unconsciously rolling her hand around on the condensation. "I'm afraid I'm a little sensitive to that seldom home business." Karen leaned back and nodded. "Probably because I'm seldom home."

She took a drink of her beer and looked sadly at Brian. For a moment there was an uncomfortable silence.

"And besides," said Brian. "I really don't want you spending hours in the kitchen cooking meals for me." He grinned when Karen rolled her eyes and smiled.

"Damn! What terrible timing," said Charlie, pulling at his beard and rolling his eyes at Natalie. "A Kodak moment, and me without my camera." He looked thoughtful.

"Let's see now, it's Friday, we've got beer—pizza's on the way—so, hey! Can we cut the bull-shit?"

They all laughed, sliding back into their normal banter, and Brian was glad to see the momentary tension eased. He left enough of that at work. Besides the television station had its demands on Karen to be met, especially lately, and the least he could offer was a little understanding while he enjoyed the time they did have together.

The pizza arrived, and when they had polished it off Karen rolled a marijuana joint that they passed around. Natalie, Charlie and Karen leaned back on the sofa, and Brian had his feet up on the slightly inclined easy chair.

"You know something?" asked Charlie. "Karen rolls a nice number. This is like a double martini at the end of a hard day. Thank you, Karen."

"You're quite welcome, Charlie. It offsets my culinary abilities somewhat."

"Why do we smoke?" asked Natalie of the room in general.

"Because it's like a martini at the end of a long hard day," answered Charlie.

"No, I mean why do we get high at all?" Natalie taught English at a junior college, and she liked clear answers to her questions. It would seem that Charlie could meet those demands since the work he did on computer programming also required precise answers, but Charlie found it easy separating the rigid structure of work from the relaxed and carefree habits of leisure.

"I get high to make less sense."

Brian laughed and said, "Good example."

"Pot leads to heroin."

"What?" Charlie asked doubtfully.

"Yes," said Natalie. "According to a recent poll, 96% of all heroin users had used pot at some time in their lives."

"Oh, OK," said Charlie. "Statistics.

"Did you know, honey," he said, "That approximately 99% of all rapists, car thieves, heroin addicts, politicians, and doggy-diddlers had milk at some time in their lives? It's disgustingly true. Take me away."

"But it's a drug."

"I don't do drugs—and none of you do, either."

"Marijuana's a drug," Natalie persisted.

"No, I don't think so. Coke, meth and heroin are drugs. Marijuana is martini."

"Even if you believe that, the pot burns our lungs, it boggles our minds, it reduces our sex drive..." Natalie shook her head.

"But it makes a person feel good," said Charlie.

"What was the question?" asked Karen. She giggled at their mock surprise.

"And you wonder why I married that woman."

"It's illegal; FDA has studied it for thirty years or so and not found a significant use for it..."

"It retards glaucoma and reduces nausea associated with radiation treatment; it relieves anxiety, especially that caused by schizophrenia," Charlie said, pulling himself to the edge of the couch—he was on a roll. "It's been medically proven to help people with multiple sclerosis and a ton of other neurological diseases. It raises the consciousness to a lower level..."

"Huh?" asked Brian.

"... and I consider this preventive maintenance."

"'Raises consciousness to a lower level?' I'm too high for this." Brian rolled his eyes and put his hands behind his head.

"What do you mean?" asked Karen.

"I mean you're more sensitive to detail, the smaller picture, the little facts that add up to the obvious whole."

Natalie jumped back in. "Would you want your pilot high while coming in for a landing at Lindberg Field? Or how about someone so high on the freeway that he can't remember why he's even on the freeway?" Brian loved it when Natalie monitored a debate. She ignored very few relevant points.

"No, of course not. I'm not glorifying pot any more than I would glorify cigarettes or alcohol. I think pot should be made legal but the user made responsible for his actions the same as if he were drinking. And no kids."

"The only thing I can see wrong with us using it," added Brian, "is that it's illegal." He remembered something Tom Short had said earlier at work. "You tell me how that makes any sense in a so-called democracy."

"Like I said before," said Charlie, "It's like that martini at the end of a loong, long hard day."

"What was the question?" asked Karen, and they all laughed again.

"Long hard day?" said Natalie. "Is that something you've read about? I wonder what your definition would be."

"Yeah, let's hear it," said Karen.

"Well, that's like getting to work ten minutes earlier than you had planned, the coffee machine is broken, spending a solid hour—and I'm not talking about any kind of break during that hour—spending a solid hour on the console, grabbing a printout wrong and getting a paper cut from it, going out to the car to drive home and noticing you've barely got enough gas to last the week." Charlie wiped a hand across his forehead. "The only thing that keeps me going is knowing I've got a smoking martini waiting for me after such a long, long, long hard day."

"Whoa!" said Brian. "I'm surprised you can make it at all."

"It's a bitch."

"Get off it," said Natalie with disbelief. "If you smoked a joint for every hard day you've ever had at work, you wouldn't even know what marijuana tasted like.

"None of us here has it better than the tall bearded one," she said to Brian while pointing at Charlie.

"Who has it the worst?" asked Karen. They all looked at Brian.

"Don't go there." Charlie groaned. "I don't want to hear another postal horror story."

"I'm with Charlie," said Brian. "I smoke to reduce the accumulated stress. There's something that will mess up your health. Stress."

"And as often as you get pissed off at work, your stress levels must be working overtime," Charlie added.

"Getting pissed off really pisses me off."

"Excellent observation," Natalie said while the others laughed. "But isn't it sometimes better to face up to a stressful situation?"

Brian sobered up and looked at Natalie. He frowned and shook his head. "That's what Tom says. He says we should fight fire with fire. But I think they're driving him crazy. Especially Whipcracker."

"I wouldn't want Tom upset with me," said Karen. "He may look like a giant teddy bear, but there's something diabolical about him."

"He's right about one thing; you can't deal with these guys on an equal basis," Brian continued. "They can do unfair things to you that you can't logically respond to. Your words don't amount to much when they are balanced against theirs. They are the bosses, after all. Normal people wouldn't take advantage, but these guys do."

"I told you not to get him started, damn it!" said Charlie. Karen smiled after him when he pulled his lanky body out of the sofa and went to the refrigerator for another beer.

"Tom's biggest problem is he tries to fight them." Brian shook his head. "He doesn't realize that it's a no win situation."

"I can't believe that you can't find a way to deal with those managers."

"Well, Natalie," said Brian. "I guess it depends on how far we are willing to go. Tom's bottom line is to shoot the bastards. I know it's just talk, but that's a very scary thought."

He paused, and they all let that sink in. "It's almost as if he has a reason for more anger at them than the rest of us. It does seem like they have singled him out lately. And for no apparent reason."

Charlie had stopped his puttering around in the kitchen to lean on the counter with a beer in his hand and a frown on his face.

"Bring me one of those beers," Brian said to him, breaking up the short silence.

"I get so tired of these horror stories," Charlie mumbled when he came back. He handed a Corona to Brian and plopped down onto the sofa. He looked at Natalie and said, "Why couldn't we have made friends with sexual deviates—wife swappers, or nudists, or someone like that?"

Natalie looked back at Brian.

"Well, Brian. I still think you should turn that stress into creative energy. You might draw up some answers to your problems at work. Even the silliest ideas would ease the tension and might actually lead to some sort of solution."

"I'll keep that in mind. But believe me when I say it's hard for us to think rationally at times. At least for me. I get so pissed off and..."

"Yeah, yeah," said Charlie. "And getting pissed off really pisses you off."

"... defensive," Brian said, grinning at Charlie, "Especially knowing that rational thought is a meaningless weapon against that bunch."

"How about that Padre's game last night?" Charlie asked Karen while leaning back and crossing his long legs.

"The main thing is not getting drawn into their traps," said Natalie. "I'm not kidding myself here. I know that it's easier for me to say than for you to do, but sometimes all an intrusively malevolent person is doing is seeking out the weaknesses in others that they can exploit. And now you're associating these local managers with the entire operations of the postal service."

"Uh oh, time to go," Charlie said to Karen as he sat back up. "Deep thinking accompanied by multi-syllabic expression makes her horny. Let's go, dear."

"Are you sure it's not just you, Charlie?" Karen asked.

"If your weaknesses, like anger and stress, aren't exposed but rather shielded by an unyielding armor of nonchalance or muted indifference, then any attack against them loses all of its force."

"Maybe we could stop at a motel on the way home." Karen punched Charlie in the arm. He stood up and chugged the nearly full bottle of beer and said, "You're driving, Natalie. My arms are sore."

"Huh. I never thought of that. It would be nice if we could come up with something, at least in our own defense, but it's not as easy as you might think," Brian said. "Like I said, I can't even explain to anyone what goes on in there. And that's a huge part of the problem—it's an indescribable, yet overwhelmingly intense feeling."

Brian stood up with the others and followed Natalie and Charlie to the door.

"Well, at least you seem to understand it more than most people do," Brian said.

"I think I get it," Natalie nodded. "And I also think you'll come up with something. When you do we'll be here to help." She frowned in thought, then added, "By the way, you should find out if there is really more going on with Tom. If he's talking about shooting people, then the thought really has crossed his mind. Without clear-cut motivation it seems extraordinarily antagonistic even given the circumstances, bad as they are."

"Wow. Can we go now?" Charlie asked. "Hope we make it to the car."

"Yeah, yeah. Get out of here. We didn't think you'd ever leave."

"We'll be back for the next exciting episode of 'Post Office Hell,'" said Charlie. "Good night!"

Chapter 2

Brian leaned over the handlebars of his Suzuki motorcycle while the cool wind drove his red hair back against his scalp. The pavement rolled smoothly beneath him. The river of traffic flowed over the coastal hills and then back into the low valleys only to climb once again in a long winding arc. Every few seconds his eyes were drawn to the serenity of the Pacific Ocean on his left. Things had gone better than usual for him all week at work, but that was going to change now.

He pulled the sleeve of his fatigue jacket from his left wrist with his teeth. He frowned, noting the time. Normally it took seventeen minutes to get from his driveway in Encinitas to the post office parking lot. But today, anyway he looked at it he was going to be late and would have to suffer the wrath of the Whip.

Supervisor Joseph P. Whipcracker as well as Supervisor of Postal Operations Phyllis Dunn, who was second in command to the postmaster, were the main instigators in the recent and unexplained conflict against the workers he'd discussed with Natalie last Friday night. Being late would only add a piece to that sudden and puzzling interest they had in heavy-handed control and discipline. At least being their target today would take the bulls-eye off of Tom for a change.

Brian shook his head. He wondered how much this recent managerial insanity had to do with the sudden current of hostilities Tom clearly harbored against their supervisors. Who had started it all? It seemed to grow out of nowhere. Sure, Tom had always been a rebel—at least from the time Brian had started working here four years ago. But he had become significantly more defiant against the managers, and even openly hostile as of late, and the growing enmity was clearly mutual.

The pavement whipped by, and Brian found himself caught up in the distraction of his thoughts. He almost didn't snap out of it in time.

A quick flash of Karen's frequent warnings to wear his helmet struck him when the two cars he was passing between at sixty-five miles per hour each began to change lanes into the one he was now occupying. The 750 cc engine responded almost to his thoughts as it roared and carried him past the perilous situation. He looked in his mirror and chuckled nervously when he saw the two cars nearly hit each other. They swerved and returned safely to their original lanes. *Ah, yes. So intent on hitting me, they almost clipped each other,* he thought. He remembered his most important rule of motorcycling, "I am invisible." It reminded him to keep his eyes open for the little traps, and its protective wisdom worked on the job as well as on the road.

*****

Brian maintained a speed of seventy-five miles per hour until he hit the Palm off-ramp. He slowed to sweep through the three quick right-hand turns that took him into the parking lot at 110 King Street where he parked and hopped off his bike. A quick glance at his watch showed him it had only taken him twelve and a half minutes today. He raced into the big, square two tone yellow building that housed the Main Post Office in Bay City. This was where most of the city's mail carriers were based; where all of the mail was sorted for delivery, and where he worked Monday through Friday, ten-thirty to seven, as the registry clerk. He threw his jacket and gloves into his locker, and hurried to the time clock next to the supervisor's duty desk to punch onto his timecard.

Whipcracker stood by the clock tapping Brian's timecard against his palm. Big silver rimmed glasses rested on his red bulbous and crater-marked nose. The color of his glass frames matched the silver and white of his immaculately groomed hair. He characteristically wore a stiff-collared, light-blue Arrow shirt and dark blue silk tie tucked into a finely creased pair of dark slacks.

None of his elaborations on style could detract from the big belly he had successfully acquired over the past thirty years of heavy beer drinking.

"Late again, huh McGraw?"

"What do you mean, 'again?'"

"This is the second time in a month you've been more than five minutes late, mister."

Wow, he thought.

"I got stopped by two female cops with an Irish fetish," he said with a grin and a shrug. When Tom Short laughed out loud from his distribution case a few feet away, Whipcracker turned to glare at him. "Come on, Joe," said Brian, winding down from the race to work. "Are you keeping a special record of me? Two times in a month? Get serious."

"I am serious!" shouted Whipcracker attracting the attention of several other clerks working in their cases near the time clock. "You're setting a pattern of delinquency by being late for work twice this month, and on top of that," he took a breath for his final thrust, "you used sixteen hours of sick leave just three weeks ago!" The pompous assessment and exaggeration of the situation would have been comical to Brian if he hadn't been stuck in the middle of it.

"You know I had the flu, and it was the first time I'd been sick in two years," said Brian, and his voice began to gain an edge as it slowly rose to a shout matching Whipcracker's roar. "And, 'setting a pattern?' Are you kidding? Only a fool could believe that two times late in a month makes a person a 'frequent tardy'. I was five minutes late when I got here, and now I'm six minutes late and still off the clock. I don't have to listen to your bullshit on my own time. So, give me my fucking time card or send me home, because you know what, Joe? All of a sudden, I don't care what you do!"

"You can't talk to me like that!"

"Sure I can, Joe." Brian spread his arms. "I'm off the clock!"

Whipcracker's face was beet red.

"Irregardless, mister, you're in big trouble." He thrust the time card into Brian's hand and turned to go, angry that his careless approach had allowed the upper hand to slip away so easily to this hot tempered Irish bastard.

"You tell him, Brian. And by the way, you mean 'regardless?'"

Whipcracker spun around to the voice as Brian punched on the clock. Tom continued throwing oversized letters into the proper pigeon holes of his flat case while glancing with a grin at Brian and then glaring at Whipcracker.

"There is no such word as 'irregardless.'" Tom rolled the word off his tongue like it made him sick.

"Short, I want to see you in the office. Now!" Whipcracker turned on his heels and headed into the assistant postmaster's office. A low murmur of familiar expectation flowed through the workroom floor.

Tom was called 'the Animal' by his friends because he seemed to be something more than mere human, not only by his six foot eight inches height and three hundred solid pounds around his bear-like paunch, but by his very nature. Either alone would have given him his title; together they reinforced it. His roguish behavior and faun-like facial features with his disconcerting flat topped studious looking black rimmed glasses lent support to the overall opinion that Tom was half animal. He wore a goatee that wrapped at the top around his upper lip in a thin mustache, and undisciplined hair that tended to grow up and flow over his scalp toward the back of his neck. He wore green tee-shirts and corduroy shorts all through the year and complained bitterly of the heat in the summer. "Darwin would have been ecstatic meeting this man," Anita de la Cruz had said.

"I want to see my steward!" he roared.

Whipcracker stuck his head back out of the assistant postmaster's office. "You don't need a steward. This is only a discussion. Now, get in here!"

"I want to see my steward!" Tom roared again. The steward represented the postal clerk-craft union—the workers—and in this case was also the union president, Bill Rose. Experience had taught Tom that a partisan witness could be very useful at these 'discussions.'

"OK, get your goddamn steward, but get in here!" Whipcracker was livid.

"Rose!"

The yell by Tom was loud enough to shake the windows, and Bill Rose, who had been working on the back dock, came racing in at the sound.

"Whipcracker?" he asked. Tom nodded his head. "Let's go." They walked into the assistant postmaster's office.

Brian went into the register cage still angry. Every day, the same old thing. Today—just a different approach. The scale of justice wasn't very balanced if he could stand up to Whipcracker, curse him out and embarrass him in front of twenty people, and walk away without any real threat of reprisal, while all that Tom had to do was look cross-eyed to find himself at odds with that vindictive and stubborn bastard. Even though Whipcracker and Tom's mutual enmity was a well-known fact here at the P. O., it still didn't give him the right to single Tom out—Tom wasn't the only one who hated the Whip.

Brian shook his head in fuming disbelief. And he had thought Tom would be safe today. Apparently Tom was never safe anymore.

"Hi, Brian."

He looked through the separation of letter throwing cases that were lined up against the other side of the crisscrossed wires that made up the wall of his registry cage.

"Hi, Jessica."

Jessica West smiled back, and Brian couldn't help himself as his eyes shot first a studious look over her magnificent body as she leaned up against her throwing chair, and then casually moved to her tanned face. Wild strawberry-blonde curls fell to her shoulders and surrounded and framed her full red lips, a delicate small nose, and emerald green eyes that were now staring back with a mixture of appreciation and amusement.

"Caught you, babe." She smiled and stretched her arms out over her head showcasing her perfect form. Brian avoided staring by turning back to work. "Oh, I don't mind when you look," she said.

"I've got some work to do," he mumbled, hoping his face wasn't as red as it felt. He hurried to the front of the cage to set up in advance his daily closeout paperwork for that evening, but not before noticing her teasing wink. She was apparently satisfied with the results of her exhibition. She was so hard to ignore, and with much effort he put his mind back to work.

*****

Despite the oppressive environment outside the cage, Brian liked the regularity of his job. Day to day he knew what his job was going to be. The other clerks could find themselves at any time either dumping dozens of heavy sacks of raw, unsorted, mail and then dividing them into separate trays of letters, and flats—like magazines—or tubs of parcels, easily the most difficult job in the post office and the one that Tom was usually assigned to; or they could end up throwing flats to separate carrier routes in a distribution case according to addresses the individual carriers delivered; or sorting letters or parcels in the same manner; taking the sorted trays of mail to the respective carriers; or even spreading to each carrier the pre-sorted bundles of PennySavers, North County news, or seasonal Mira Costa College schedules assigned to individual routes for delivery.

Very random, impulsively assigned jobs.

Sometimes a distribution clerk was singled out for the pleasant duty of delivering, by jeep, special deliveries or express mail into the community. The beauty of this job was that it took them out of the dramas of the office for a few hours. Unfortunately, assignment of all of this work was left to the discretion of a supervisor who much too frequently let his nature and disposition be his guide.

But such was the normal life of most postal clerks—irregular duties and chores, done behind the scenes with little appreciation or recognition.

Brian's job also included checking all of the carriers in at night as they brought back either the signed delivery slips or the undelivered accountable mail to the office. The carriers were checked out every morning by Edwin "the Caribbean Cannonball" Fernandez, the morning registry clerk, with vehicle keys, dog spray, and of course the CODs, registered and certified letters, postage due and express mail—items they had to put their John Hancock to—making each of them accountable for these things before they could take them to the street.

Then Edwin threw mail in the late morning with the other clerks while Brian took over the cage. Atomic flatulations had given Edwin his nickname. After starting work at 3:30 in the morning Edwin went home at noon unless he was forced to work overtime.

Brian also periodically collected incoming registered mail from the windows up front during the day as it came into the office from customers. He added each collection to his register list for dispatch to the district post office in San Diego in the evening.

The front window visits had lately given him an opportunity to observe one of the window clerks, Teeth, in action, something he enjoyed immensely and always found worth a laugh. He thought the guy should be performing at the Comedy Store. But even when he wasn't 'on,' it seemed his customers were. And between Teeth and his customers, Brian found time to overlook the mounting absurdities of the back for at least a few pleasant moments.

The registers that Brian collected and sent to San Diego on the last collection truck of the evening were processed by a register clerk in San Diego for further cross-country or world-wide distribution. These and the other regular portions of his job kept him busy most of the day. And he had weekends off—two days in a row—a luxury most clerks in Bay City didn't have.

It may have been occasionally challenging, but it was thankfully a busy and routine job. The time always seemed to fly by as he worked. An added plus was that the supervisors—such as Whipcracker and Lenny (the Weasel) Nicks—seldom gave him a hard time because of the nature of his work. Now Brian found himself somewhere between a clerk and a supervisor in the postal family caste system of respectability. He liked that very much. For the most part he was invisible.

Brian moved to the C.O.D. section of the cage and began writing C.O.D. second notices.

"Brian," Jessica whispered through the screen. "I didn't mean to embarrass you."

"You didn't embarrass me." He avoided eye contact, knowing she would embarrass him again.

"Do you think he'll get in trouble this time?"

"Who—Tom? I don't know."

"I thought you were in trouble this morning, but you handled it nicely. Told that fucker off, didn't you?"

Brian glanced at her quickly, then back to his paper work. Her salty language still occasionally took him by surprise although that contrasting innocent-brassy comportment seemed to emanate naturally from her.

"Yeah, thanks. Usually they all stay off my back because they don't know what I do in here anyway."

"I don't know what you do in there."

Brian laughed. That ignorance of his job had kept all of the more senior employees from putting in for the register cage when it went up for bid. They apparently didn't realize how much it would keep the supervisors off their backs—a day like today being the exception.

"And I don't understand why Tom is always getting into trouble. Even if he is a giant asshole," she added.

"Me either," said Brian.

"Seems like everyone's getting in more trouble lately."

"I agree."

"Well, I'm taking a break now," Jessica said as she slid off her lean-to. "Would you care to come along?"

"I can't," said Brian sheepishly. "I just got to work." The effect she had on him was amazing.

"Well, then," she smiled and added in her best husky Austrian accent as she leaned toward the wire wall, "I'll be back!"

Brian continued writing notices after glancing after her retreating figure. He tried to put his mind back on his work, but when it moved away from her it trailed off to the fresh conflict in the office.

As much as he'd been thinking about it lately, he still couldn't figure out the ridiculous division that had slowly grown between management and labor. They were all supposed to be working together—right?—one goal. The people he worked with were OK; the jobs weren't that difficult once they were learned, and employees soon became productive experts at what they did. So it didn't make sense; he couldn't understand why there were so many clashes. At times he wondered if it was his own prejudicial attitude that had him thinking management was responsible for this split. But here was the rational to that thought again—Tom was still on the carpet in the assistant postmaster's office for saying something that didn't suit Whipcracker's momentary disposition.

"Bullshit!" floated clearly through the walls to the cage. The door to the offices banged open, and Tom stormed out. "You're a liar; I never threatened you!" he shouted as he stood by the time clock.

"Short, I want you off the clock this minute." Red was becoming Whipcracker's color of the day. He was even shaking now.

"Goddamn it! That's bullshit! If I was going to strike you, it wouldn't have been just a threat." Tom suddenly leaned toward Whipcracker. "As a matter of fact..."

"Tom, Tom." Bill Rose stepped in with an urgent peace-keeping hand held high. "If he wants you to take a vacation, take it. You'll get paid."

"The hell he will!" shouted Whipcracker. "You'll get no vacation from me! I know a threat when I see one!"

"Don't worry," said Bill. "We'll take care of it."

Tom looked at Bill for a moment and slowly began to relax. After all, Bill was the steward and local union president. Tom figured he must know what he was talking about. He glared back at Whipcracker and said, "You guys are always trying to screw me with your lies, aren't you? That's on top of losing all my damn leave chits. Well, don't come looking for me when you want me back." He punched off the clock and stared at Whipcracker before adding, "Some of us are capable of taking care of ourselves." He stared a moment longer and then stormed away toward the rear of the post office.

Whipcracker scowled at Tom's huge back and then at Bill before he turned and headed toward the postmaster's office to discuss with the reclusive postmaster, Henry Whynaught, Tom's "threats and insubordination." "Threats" wasn't as common as "insubordination" as passwords to discipline by management, but either of them alone or together was usually enough of a catchall to satisfy the vindictive pleasures of a tyrannical supervisor. It was similar to "silent contempt" being grounds for discipline in the military. Whipcracker would now plead the case to the postmaster who would naturally take the Whip's side—the side of management; a letter of discipline would be filed against Tom Short, by Whipcracker, and the union would step in to defend Tom. One step now-a-days followed the other.

Brian had watched the action by the time clock, and familiar anger burned inside of him as he turned back to his work.

Why couldn't Whipcracker take a joke? That's all that Tom intended originally; sure, maybe a little dig. But why did Whipcracker think he was so unapproachably superior to Tom? Why did any supervisor think they were so fucking superior? They all used to work as either clerks or carriers until the power of leadership was placed in their hands. No one challenged their right to supervise—that was never the problem. *And the only difference between supervisors like Whipcracker and the Weasel and employees like Tom Short and me is that they had volunteered for the job, and we hadn't.*

Although it had only begun, Brian couldn't wait for this day to end. The ride home on his motorcycle always had a meditative effect on him as the wind whipped through his hair sweeping his frustrations into the air and dispelling his antagonisms for another day.

Brian looked at his watch. Karen was probably starting work, he thought. He remembered the look in her eyes two months ago when she announced, with great flourish, that she had been given the noon anchor job at "KMAA, Channel 7; the television station coming to you from beautiful downtown San Diego, America's finest city." The announcement had come over the flickering candlelight at Friar Tuck's where she had taken him for a celebration dinner.

The ratings took a mild jump shortly thereafter and pulled the KMAA noon news to a competitive level with the other two major stations in San Diego. Karen had never been happier. This is what she had studied for at San Diego State where she and Brian had first met, and this is what she had worked for the last three years at KMAA, first in the copy and editing room, and finally as a street reporter sniffing out criminal and human interest stories to report on the air. Her popularity on the air became evident to the station owner and manager, Donnie Bonito.

Her appointment to the noon anchor was a story in itself: When KMAA reported the embezzlement of station collected charity funds against them by their previous noon news anchorman, Dave Rump, "put the news behind you with Dave Rump," the story was reported out of conscientious editorial necessity and with suitable regret by Karen McGraw. One week later, Donnie officially made her Rump's replacement.

Even then she wasn't satisfied with her enviable position. After getting the noon anchor she seemed to be lately doubling her efforts to climb the ladder, spending less and less time with Brian, and much more time covering and delivering stories on the evening and late news.

The climb to this level had been accomplished through her hard work, but now it was becoming even tougher on Brian as their time together continued to diminish.

"Anchoring the evening news is my goal, Brian. And I feel that I'm almost there." Karen had been explicit knowing that her honesty was important to him. They may see less of each other for a short time, she said, but the results would soon enough be profitable in quality time and financial security. The people she worked with loved her; her audience loved her.

Brian date-stamped the forms on his counter top.

Sure, it was tough waiting. But if anyone was worth waiting for, it was Karen. And for a second pleasant time in a week, she had arranged to be home tonight and, *Horrors!* he thought, had planned on cooking supper.

Brian grinned thinking about what disaster she'd be cooking up.

He had to admit, he enjoyed the recent notoriety of being Karen McGraw's husband. He had few doubts about the strength of their relationship, but he was human, and those he had were as easily dispelled by Karen as hers were by him. The superior-inferior, male or female dominant complexes had never edged their way into this relationship. In college, they had become very good friends before they had discovered their mutually deep love and sexual attraction for each other, or at least before they had chosen to do anything about it. Karen enjoyed Brian's friends, and now Brian found himself as often floating on Donnie Bonito's enormous forty-nine foot sailboat as going to a Padre's baseball game with Charlie Sharp, who had been another college buddy—one he had met before Karen—and who was now a computer programming wizard at a Sorrento Valley software company.

Brian spent most of the day sifting through an active collage of dreams and reality, wondering how he could make this a less stressful job, wondering when he would be able to spend more time on Donnie Bonito's sailboat—or his own if he had one—alone with Karen, wondering what the hell would happen to Tom Short, now; wondering what was going on in Whipcracker's head, if anything, wondering, oddly, what Whipcracker's parents were like, and wondering how such a person could possibly well serve the human race or this planet. To his revulsion, Whipcracker continually penetrated his thoughts.

*****

The coolness of the evening ocean breezes whipped at him, chilling him as Brian headed home to Encinitas in the dark on his Suzuki 750. After seven o'clock, most of the rush hour traffic had died down, but he noticed there were more cars on the freeway now than there had been only a few years ago. It was early September, but colder than usual, and he reminded himself as his knees rattled against his gas tank to carry long johns to work for the evening ride home tomorrow.

He pulled into the fast lane to pass a slower moving group of cars, and as he neared his exit a diaper service panel truck moved in tightly behind him with its bright lights on. Brian waved his left hand to ask the driver to back off. The man gave him the finger from his lit up interior and pulled closer, to within a few inches of his back wheel. Brian couldn't move from his position in traffic because he had already inched up to the car in front to create more space between himself and the truck when he spotted its quick approach in his rear view mirror.

The interior light showed the driver wearing a malevolent grin. Brian could not think of a logical reason why that man would be endangering his life. Perhaps at some time his wife had been caught fooling around with someone who rode a shining black motorcycle like his own, and he felt that this was his opportunity for revenge.

Well, fuck him, thought Brian whose quick Irish temper had been slowly overcoming his fear of this impending danger. He reached into the cup he had placed long ago in the brake wires by his handlebars and grabbed out the three marble-sized ball bearings that he'd never before had cause to use. He couldn't even remember what had possessed him to put them there in the first place. But today was not a good day for that diaper service driver to be testing the waters of that curiosity.

They slowly inched by the cars on the right. He saw his chance and flung the ball bearings over his shoulder and into the windshield of the panel truck. He pulled quickly through the traffic to the coming exit and swept off the freeway as the truck driver banged his horn, flashed his lights and failed to get over in time to take the same exit.

Explain that to your boss, Brian thought. *And I hope that guy's still fucking your wife.*

Karen had kept her promise and been home since five-thirty. Supper was burning on the stove when Brian came into the house. He threw his helmet and gloves into the hall closet, and sniffed at the smoke.

"Salmon?"

"Veal Parmesan."

Brian watched her scrape at the meat that had welded itself to the frying pan.

"Pizza?" he asked hopefully.

"Sure, I'll buy." She dumped the frying pan in the sink, meat intact, and walked up to Brian to give him a lingering kiss.

"You been messing with that motorcycling mailman again?" he asked as he raised an eyebrow.

"Sure, but I thought we had an understanding," she teased. "Maybe I can do something to make it up to you," she said while playing with the zipper on his jacket. Brian put his hands under her blouse and caressed her back. She drew closer and said, "C-c-cold!"

"OK," he laughed as he stepped back. "Warm pizza first, you frigid bitch. And then unbridled sex!"

She laughed as she threw on her jacket from the closet. "Pretty cocky, aren't you? Maybe I won't tell you the good news. At least until you come through for me." Brian reached out to her again and started to slide his hands into her jacket and under her blouse. "OK, OK," she laughed as she wrestled his hands away. "I'll talk."

"Too easy," he said. "I was just getting warmed up."

"Bullshit," she shivered. She spoke quickly when his hands started toward her again. "We've got the boat this weekend, and I'm not working Saturday or Sunday. Donnie Bonito and his cute little boyfriend are going to Tahoe to play in the snow they insist will be there. And Natalie and Charlie said they'd like to go sailing with us, too. Charlie called just before you got home."

"All right!" Brian went to the phone on the dining room wall and began to dial Charlie. "That's great. I can use some peace and quiet." He lowered the phone. "It was pretty bad at work today. Some of those turkeys have become bigger and bigger pains in the ass lately." Karen liked to keep up to date on developments, pleasing her newscaster's curiosity. "The Whip sent Tom Short home early for threatening him today."

"When are those two getting married?" asked Karen.

"I think Tom's starting to crack—he keeps talking seriously about buying a gun to blow Whipcracker away."

"Oh, my God! He's still talking like that? He scares me sometimes. He's so intimidating! I don't want to be reporting anything like that on the news."

"Ha-row?" said the voice on the phone.

"Hi, Charlie. Turning Japanese?"

"*Ohayo*, Brian," said Charlie-san. "We hov boat for weeken?"

"OK, Charlie. For one thing, it's night, not morning. For another, and I hate to break this to you, you are not Japanese." Charlie gasped on the other end. "Yes, it's true. You're too tall and ugly. I warned you about buying that imported computer."

"OK, OK!" he cried. "I can take it!" Then in a perfectly calm, low voice, "Vee got zee boot?"

"Ya, vee got zee boot. Karen and I are going out for pizza, if you guys care to join us."

"Thanks, anyway," said Charlie. "But Natalie and I are eating already. We're having sushi and Lowenbrau."

They made plans to meet Saturday at Donnie Bonito's slip to sail to Catalina and then back again on Sunday. Charlie loved to sail as much as Brian did. Being a computer wizard, he loved to bring his technical mind to sport against the unpredictable elements of the sea. He was so different away from the terminals he was such an expert on. The rougher the seas, the more he was in his glory as he manned the wheel in Donnie's forty-nine footer with his orange slicker blowing in the wind, and his eyes blazing and his beard soaked, looking like a tall, lanky Captain Ahab. Unfortunately for Charlie's sailor ego, the coastal waters from Baja to Los Angeles were usually as smooth as a baby's skin with only an occasionally serious blow.

Karen and Natalie loved the ocean as much as their husbands did. Natalie would trade off with Brian in the galley while Karen frequently hauled sail for the captain, unanimously banished as she was from the galley. When sails and course were set, they'd relax and find spots on deck to sun "two of the most gorgeous bodies on the high seas at any time," as Charlie would say to an appreciably nodding and admiring Brian. Out here they could wear those tiny, almost transparent bikinis—the ones you usually only see in Sports Illustrated annual swimsuit issues, or travelogues from Rio—without gathering the careless stares of muscle-bound beach junkies who stumbled over each other in their distraction. Here it was only the leering eyes of Captain Ahab and Mr. Christian, brought together by their desirable cargo.

Brian would never forget the two times in the past when the girls had mutually decided to remove their bikini tops so they could catch "a few extra rays in a few different places." He and Charlie had made little of those pleasurable moments in the hope that their nonchalance would lead to a frequent occurrence of the thrilling exhibition.

*****

"Land ho," hollered Charlie from the helm an hour after they had set sail from the Bay City Harbor. Donnie Bonito had equipped his huge boat, the Columbo, for single-handed sailing, and Brian grinned from where he sat with his arms resting on the edges of the cockpit as he watched Charlie maneuver for a tack. The tiny dot of Catalina was still at least eight hours away.

"Coming About!" he shouted to the women below. Natalie was making coffee to warm them up in the blustery unseasonable September cold. No bikinis today, thought Brian sadly as Charlie completed his tack and the wind once more filled the sails.

"I'm afraid to ask, but, what the hell? How are things at the old P.O.?" asked Charlie.

"Same old shit," said Brian, sitting up. "You start doing well at something to satisfy your personal drive for perfection, like sorting eight feet of letter mail in an hour when the average is five and a half, and it becomes your new personal standard. You fall below your arbitrary standard, and you're disciplined. You know my supervisors, Charlie." Charlie nodded. "They're useless except for telling the complaining public 'that's the way it is, sorry ma'am,' or handing out discipline to the employees just to show you who's the boss. Seems like customer satisfaction used to come first; seems like hard work used to be appreciated if not rewarded."

"Seems like something happened again this week."

"Yeah, but not to me. Just the usual mental wrestling with Whipcracker who, as you know, has the brains of a tuna fish. No—what happened was Tom Short got sent home from work Thursday. He's such an easy mark in his self-righteousness, and he and Whipcracker really hate each other. Anyway, when it comes down to management's word against one of its employees—that's me, Charlie—you know who's right."

"Management," agreed Charlie as he shook his head. "Why don't you get a real job? When I have trouble with management, I tell them I'm going to fuck up their computer for the next six months and sell our secrets to the Russians, and they back right off. Now that's the American Way."

"Sure. I wish we had an outlet. Overall, we can't so much as strike against unfair labor practices or we're fired. We can't criticize the Postal Service, even to the end of bettering it by showing up deficiencies, because we would be in violation of the Postal Service Code of Ethics that declares something like conduct that reflects unfavorably upon the Postal Service is an act of disloyalty, given a gray area here and there.

"Furthermore, we have to follow every direct order given to us, no matter how stupid or illegal it is, unless it puts us in an unsafe predicament, or we are disciplined for disobeying a direct order. Article Three of our National Agreement. Even if we're right and we win our case by grieving it, we lose for disobeying a direct order. You figure it out. Management has the right to mismanage, and you ain't got doodily-squat. I think that's the exact wording of Article Three."

"Now that really sucks, man. Sheet. Gotdamn. Mutha-fucka. Matta fack, tam to kick a mutha-fucka's ass, man. Sheet, bro. Tam to slit a mutha-fucka's tars, man. Slit some tars! I's pissed!" He rocked back and forth at the helm, eyes blazing.

Brian studied him. "Who are you now?"

Charlie looked hurt. "Bobcat Billy Bob Willie Boy Johnson...Junior."

"My god; there's a senior?"

"And four more juniors, actually; back in ole Swamp Hollar. I's Junior, the third."

"I think Tom Short has a better idea, Junior, the third. He wants to take a riot gun and blow away da mudda-fuckas. He thinks he's a Molly McGuire."

"Uh-oh," said Charlie as Natalie came topsides holding a lit marijuana cigarette burnt half way down. "Time to get serious."

"Look what Donnie left next to the coffee," she said. She giggled as she handed it to Brian.

Karen laughed and blinked into the sunlight coming up. "Always looking out for our welfare," she said.

*****

They all sat comfortably with jackets on and collars lifted against the penetrating wind as they passed the joint around. Charlie had set them on an economical course that required little more work than a hand on the wheel and they sat in the warmth of friendship listening to the wind in the rigging, the slaps of water on the boat, and the whispers of nature found only in the deepest forests or miles from shore.

"This is what it's all about," said Brian, and the others felt his words more than heard them. "This is the big payoff for all the organized bullshit. Let's never go back."

*****

?

A blast of wind found its way under the thick canopy of dark, giant trees. Lenny pulled his jacket around his neck against the chill. He looked at the imposing red-brick building and back at his car. Today it looked like he'd plowed into the setting of a nightmarish fairy tale, and here he was to meet the wicked witch.

God, he hated these visits. He was tempted to climb back in and drive away, but what kind of a son would that make him? Besides, he could always use these confrontations to build up a little fire to take into work and spread among the pieces of shit that worked for him. He hated those assholes even more than his own mom; and they were even easier to push around. He thought about

Jimmy Winfield and his scowl deepened. Well, maybe not always. That lucky motherfucker nearly cost him his job.

He kicked at a stone in the unpaved parking lot before he headed toward the front entrance, his hitched up step betraying his anxieties.

He walked reluctantly down the sanitized hallway, hesitating at a door before taking a deep breath and shoving it open. The old lady sitting on the mussed-up bed looked like a survivor of a concentration camp when she whipped the thin strands of her hair around to lay her wild-eyed gaze upon him.

"Oh, joy. My kid. Yay."

"Ma." He stepped in and stood near a chair while looking down at her. "Always a pleasure."

She stared at him suspiciously.

"Get me out of here."

Lenny laughed.

"So you can blow the rest of Pa's life insurance on the crazy crap you were spending it on?"

"It's my money!"

"Right."

She looked at him, blinking her eyes.

"I'm your Ma."

"You're a drunk who has lost her mind."

She snapped her head back to glare at him.

"You're a bad, bad son." He frowned and shook his head slowly, just as disgusted by her. "You're a weasel, just like the little girl said."

"What?" He stepped closer to her. When she said nothing he suddenly grabbed her shoulders and shook her. "What did you say?"

At first a look of fright crossed her eyes. But that look changed when she realized the power she had conjured over his emotions with that one word.

"Weasel," she said, smiling. "She said they called you the weasel."

"Who said that?"

"Let go of me! Nurse! Help!"

Lenny released her, and a nurse came rushing into the room.

"Everything OK? She looked from one to the other. Mrs. Nicks was grinning at her son.

"He grabbed me," she said, rubbing her thin shoulders, but she did not look threatened. As a matter of fact, the son looked more flustered than the mom.

"Did you?"

"Of course not," he said, slumping into the bedside chair. "You know how she gets."

"I'm not crazy, you know."

"Well." The nurse was confused.

"We're all right!" Lenny snapped.

The nurse frowned at Lenny, then said to Mrs. Nicks, "I'll be nearby if you need anything." She slowly pulled the door shut as she backed out.

Lenny looked at his mom, who was still grinning that maniacal, superior tooth-gapped grin. She mouthed, "Weasel."

"That girl here, Ma?"

"She said she used to work for you; that you weren't the worst of the bunch that drove her crazy; but they all called you weasel behind your back. Weasel?" She laughed. "They must really love you."

He wasn't listening to the scraggily bitch anymore. It had dawned on him who that "little girl" was. He couldn't remember her name, but he remembered all the crap they had put her through. All for Whipcracker, too. They shouldn't have done it, but it had actually turned out to be fun for him. He hated all of them. None of them had any respect. And she was here in this loony bin with his crazy mom?

He stood up thinking "the weasel" wasn't the worst of them, huh? We'll see about that. After all those jerks did to screw up his advancement? Tom Short; the black kid, Jimmy, and his EEO bullshit; that stinking instigator McGraw with his above it all attitude? That little girl might be the key to showing all of those sniveling whiners why he was the one blessed with the suit and tie and why they were the lowlifes taking the orders. God, he hated them. Every fucking one of them. He couldn't get that out of his head. Whipcracker was right, though. You take down one, hard, and they all fall. And Tom Short was the obvious target, now, seeing how Whipcracker hated him more than any of the others.

"Where you going?"

He opened the door and she said, a little desperately, "You just got here."

He shut the door, and had only taken a few steps down the sterile hallway when he heard her screech, "Weasel! You weasel! Come back here!"

He wondered where the girl was being confined. Maybe she would be more receptive to a sweet, contrite Lenny now. The nurse gave him a cautious, distrustful look as she scampered past him, but he ignored her. "Oh, I'll be back, you witch," he thought, his eyes flicking around. "Now that there's someone here I want to see."

Chapter 3

Wednesday morning Ramon Lopez watched from his distribution case as Supervisors Whipcracker and Lenny Nicks headed toward the assistant postmaster's office. They whispered something over by Brian's register cage that brought chuckles and wicked smirks from each before they casually slunk into the office.

"Sucker even looks like a weasel, don't he?"

Ramon turned to see Jimmy Winfield glaring at his nemesis Lenny "the Weasel" Nicks from his own distribution case.

"He's acted like one long enough. Yeah; he is a weasel."

"I agree," said Anita de la Cruz from her nearby letter sorting case.

"I wonder what those two are up to now. You know when they happy, they out to screw somebody." Jimmy knew about that firsthand. He'd been given two letters of warning and a suspension of one week by the Weasel over a year ago, and the Weasel wasn't even his supervisor. He was a carrier supervisor who hated anyone taller, better looking, or smarter than himself, and that took in just about everyone. The Weasel had been in his glory knowing that Jimmy couldn't do anything about the discipline he'd been issued because as everyone already knew or would learn in time, when it came right down to a supervisor's word against a worker's in the union grievance process, the supervisor nearly always won and especially so if he had been discreet in his presentation, something these guys had become great at.

So Jimmy said, "Fuck that shit," and went instead to EEO, Equal Employment Opportunity, where his opportunity for a fair shake was greatly improved, and he had little trouble proving that reprisal and race were factors in the Weasel's discipline, since the Weasel discriminated against everyone, and since the Weasel couldn't defend himself against the penetrating questions of a non-biased attorney-examiner without exposing himself as the vindictive immature weasel that he was.

Jimmy Winfield smiled thinking about how he had finally won his case. Management had ended up with egg on its face for defending the little prick Weasel. Jimmy won his one week back pay and had all records of discipline officially expunged from all of his files "never to be used against him again." It took nearly a year to clear up that suspension, and it had made him happy, but he was more than a little disillusioned with a management that could have settled the problem within the office if they hadn't been so weak and bending to the whimsical lies of one supervisor. The fact that it cost the postal service $6,482.00 just to lose this case caused the elusive Postmaster Henry Whynaught to issue the order to all supervisors that Jimmy Winfield was off limits. But Jimmy was still pissed off.

"They've been riding Tom a lot lately," said Ramon as he stood with a handful of magazines and watched the door where Whipcracker and the Weasel had disappeared.

Tom Short had only come back to work this morning from his suspension. The postmaster had finally reached him on Tuesday to let him know that he was required back at work. Tom had kept his promise to lay low by heading off to his mysterious Mexican village, and now the postal service owed him for the time he had been off work since being taken off the clock Thursday by Whipcracker. He had been issued a Notice of Suspension when he came into work, a suspension that really could be carried out in a couple of weeks, but Bill Rose said that it would be grieved, and there was nothing to be done about it for now. Administrative Leave, as explained to Whipcracker by the postmaster and Bill Rose, could only be carried out without pay when in conjunction with an emergency suspension, so Tom would get paid, as promised by Bill, for the time he'd already been off. An angry Whipcracker had been given a rare and ill-received lecture by Postmaster Whynaught on the coordination of postal operations and human relations within its structure, and Whipcracker used it as fuel to fire the hatred he already held for Tom Short.

Tom had been sent out to the dock to dump mail in the morning chill. Ramon knew that he had been sent out of the way so he wouldn't realize this meeting was taking place. Tom, none the wiser, was relishing the cold against his bare legs and arms as he worked in his corduroy shorts and green tee-shirt.

"I can't understand what the point is in their attacks on the Animal," said Ramon. "He's a free spirit; why can't they let him be?"

"He's different," said Anita. "And some people can't leave those who are different alone."

"Shh... check this out," said Jimmy as the clerks continued casing the mail in their hands. Darrell Diamond, the other carrier supervisor, and Phyllis Dunn, the assistant postmaster, walked by them and into Phyllis's office closing the door behind them. Now all four of them were in there.

"They out to fuck somebody," said Jimmy as he shook his head. "Sure wish I knew what they was talking about."

"Me, too," Ramon said as he grinned and went back to throwing mail. He knew he'd hear soon enough—as soon as he removed the little tape recorder he'd planted in there at two-thirty in the morning when he came to work. He had heard key words yesterday indicating this meeting would take place as he eavesdropped on Diamond talking to Whipcracker, and he had planted the expensive voice activated tape recorder under Phyllis's desk before any of the supervisors had arrived. That little mail order recorder was only one part of his elusive ability to be in the right place at the right time and he was the official keeper of the closets—Ramon Lopez knew where all the skeletons hung.

Brian walked out of the locker room, past the swing room to the time clock and waited to punch on. He looked at Ramon and pointed at the door leading to the offices.

Ramon nodded his head. "They're all in there."

"I wondered where the hell they were. When they get secretive, you know they're getting ready to screw someone."

"See, Ramon? You got it, brother," said Jimmy to Brian. "They gonna fuck somebody."

Suddenly a man in a window clerk's uniform dashed past the register cage from the direction of the front window to where Brian, Ramon and Jimmy were talking. He looked them over, then grabbed Brian's arm and turned him confidentially away from the other two.

"All right. I'm going to make this brief. You single, man?"

"Who the hell are you?" asked Brian as he pulled his arm free. Ramon, Anita and Jimmy were watching with wide eyes.

"I think he likes you," said Jimmy.

"OK, so you're married. We'll be discreet. But this is an emergency."

Brian said, "Touch me again, and I'll kick your ass from here to the Bay City Pier." Ramon laughed.

"What's wrong with you guys? You a bunch of fags? I've got a Bo Derek look-alike up at the front counter who can't go out with me unless I get a date for her Swedish cousin."

"Fags...!" said Anita de la Cruz. "What kind of homophobic...?"

"Swedish cousin?" bellowed Tom Short as he came in from the dock to take his ten minute break in the swing room. "Blonde?"

"Yes. You seem like a reasonable—huge—man," said the stranger as he stepped over quickly to look up at Tom. "Can you be here at five-thirty tonight?"

"Be here!"

"Good. We'll pick up the goddesses at six, and be home by twelve."

"Swedish goddesses?"

"Oh, yeah! Be here at five-thirty, Big Foot. Gotta get back— we've got a line out the door. Five-thirty!" With that the stranger was gone.

Jimmy and Brian stood shaking their heads slowly in amazement as Ramon laughed again. Tom was mumbling about blonde Swedish goddesses as he sauntered into the swing room.

"Who the hell was that bigoted asshole?" asked Anita.

"That," said the all-knowing Ramon, "Was Earnie Franks, our new window clerk as of today. The guy who's taking Bob Higgins' and Teeth's place on the window."

"Well, I already don't like him."

"You're kidding," said Brian. "He's the one that management was keeping such a big secret about?"

"Have you seen his personnel file?" asked Jimmy.

"Not yet," said Ramon with a sly grin that they all recognized. "But check this out. I have a cousin who works for a glass company up in L. A. who told me a little bit about him that you might find interesting. Matter-of-fact, it's the reason he's here—a direct transfer. While replacing some broken windows at a huge post office up there, my cousin asked the postmaster how the windows got broken."

Brian punched on the clock and started writing up second notices on C.O.D.s in the reg-cage because they were something he had to do, and because they kept him close enough to Ramon to hear him as he told his story.

"The postmaster who hired Miguel to put in the new window panes blew up when Miguel asked him about the broken glass."

"Miguel?" Anita asked.

"His cousin," Jimmy frowned impatiently. "Go on."

"Miguel couldn't believe the reaction he got. The postmaster got real pissed off at the question. He turned red and started sputtering, you know, not really saying anything. He kept throwing his hands up like he wanted to say something, but he could only sputter. He finally left the room, sputtering, and Miguel figured it was to have a heart attack or something. Of course, now Miguel was really curious. He asked the regular maintenance guy who came by a little while later, when he was almost finished with the glass, to please tell him what the hell had happened here."

Ramon paused in his mail throwing and shook his head. Brian, Anita and Jimmy anxiously waited. They knew a revealing excerpt of the new man's history was being unfolded, and they savored every word hoping to know more about the whirlwind that had just passed through.

"The maintenance man said, it was the weirdest thing; that out of nowhere the postmaster started picking up paperweights, chairs, the telephone, and began throwing them all around the office, against the walls and through the windows. Wrapped himself up in a rage; threw a regular fit. Like a madman. Turned out that our new window clerk had been banging his wife."

"Earnie Franks!" said Brian and Jimmy.

"That's right. Now get this; he told the postmaster himself!"

"What? What balls," Jimmy said.

"He didn't know she was the postmaster's wife. Didn't know she was anybody's wife. This really blew Miguel away. Seems Earnie had asked for a long weekend to coincide with that of this mysterious woman he'd been meeting under secretive circumstances. They were going to Palm Springs," Ramon laughed. "But this Earnie, he's got to brag all about what he planned for her that weekend to the postmaster who finally deduced who she was. That's when the P.M. flipped out. Gal never told Ernie that she was married."

"He had to know," said Anita.

"The maintenance man said the postmaster had been recovering nicely until Miguel had somehow stirred it all up again with his question. Bottom line is Mr. Earnie Franks has been transferred without loss of seniority for the good of the postal service. But I guess the ghost lives on, eh?"

Brian laughed and said, "Guess who got the ghost?"

"Hey, this man might be all right after all," said Anita. "Let's introduce him to Weasel's wife."

"Yeah!" said Jimmy.

They were still talking and laughing when the secret meeting broke up and Whipcracker stepped out of the office.

"Hey! Knock off the chattering. I think there's enough work around here to keep your mouths shut and your hands moving."

"Yeah, bowse," drawled Jimmy as Ramon and Brian snickered. They'd heard Jimmy say before, "They think I'm their nigger, all the better for me. Talking that trash takes them off guard, and there ain't much better defense than being underestimated. Besides, it really pisses them off." They hadn't slowed down their work while Ramon told his story, but that didn't matter much to the Whip.

"Think that's funny?" asked Whipcracker. Diamond and Weasel stepped out of the office and stood to watch. "I'll tell you what's funny. Two hours of mandatory overtime. Now that's funny."

"Thanks, bowse," said Jimmy. "You one hell of a sport. Think I can work ten hours on my day off, too?"

Whipcracker turned red, and Diamond and Weasel turned to walk away after lending looks of condescending disapproval to the situation.

"Hey, I'm a little short on money and dwarfed by a particular six thousand dolla' bill," said Jimmy to Weasel's back with the emphasis on 'short' and 'dwarfed'. "One of my shortcomings is that very large legal bill. Thanks for the overtime, boss man." He would never let Weasel forget about his expensive EEO loss and his own immunity or Weasel's size.

"Get to work, and shut-up," hollered Whipcracker.

"Yeah, bowse." Jimmy smiled as he began throwing mail. He'd seen the hitch in Weasel's step, and he knew with satisfaction that he had again pissed him off.

"Show us your very large bill," said Ramon in a low voice as Brian laughed. Whipcracker had walked over to the swing room door.

"How long of a break are you taking?" Whipcracker asked.

"I've only been in here five minutes," growled Tom. "How would you know how long I've been in here?"

"I think it's been long enough. Get back out on the dock."

"I'm taking a ten minute break like everyone else. So why don't you get the hell out of the swing room? It's for real workers!"

"What's this? A threat?"

"You and your goddamn threats!" roared Tom. "Arrgh!" He got up and headed for the dock. He had already been served notice of suspension once today, and couldn't very well argue with the idiot after that. All he could do was growl.

"What's that?" asked Whipcracker. "Got something you want to say?" Tom was not so caught up in his fury when he turned around that he didn't see Brian nodding toward the assistant postmaster's office. Phyllis Dunn was peeking out, and when Tom saw that, he said in a low-rumbling and ominous voice, "Time's not right." He ignored Whipcracker's request to repeat that and headed out to the dock to dump mail. Union President Bill Rose stopped Tom momentarily as he came in to take his own break, and Tom nodded before going outside. Whipcracker had walked back into Phyllis's office on her hand signal, and Rose spoke with Ramon in low tones.

Anita slid off her stool and said, "Let's see them stop me from taking my break!" She strolled into the swing room with an angry stare toward the offices.

"Jimmy, Brian," Bill said, turning to them from Ramon. "Can you make a special meeting tomorrow night?"

"Sure," said Brian. "What's up?"

"I think we'd better wait until then. The walls have ears." Rose looked around. "Spread the word." Then he disappeared into the swing room to take his break.

"I can't wait to hear this," said Brian, not knowing whether it would be good news or bad.

"Must be some important shit," said Jimmy. "I ain't missing it. If it's got anything to do with screwing the Weasel, you can count me in."

If it's got anything to do with balancing the scales of justice, thought Brian, *you can count me in.* A plan had been hatching in his head for several days now, probably in part to his and Natalie's discussion, Tom's removal from the workroom floor Thursday, and his own run-in with Whipcracker. He thought that tomorrow night's meeting might be the right time to present it.

*****

Later on Brian walked into the swing room for a short break. Most of the clerks, with their two hours of mandatory overtime, were taking their last break of the day. Teeth was imparting final farewells—the Spring Valley supervisory job was officially his, and he was on his way out of Bay City.

"We're going to miss you, Teeth." Brian shook his hand. "That Spring Valley job will suit you fine. Don't mess up, and make sure you come back to replace one of these assholes someday." Brian sat down at the long swing room table.

"And make it soon," added Jessica as she shook his hand. "I've got to ask you—what's your real name, Teeth?"

Teeth grinned the big toothy grin that had given him his nickname, and said, "Supervisor Mark Adrienne Simpson at your future service, young lady, because I shall be back."

"Yeah? Well, don't fuck up, Mark Adrienne Simpson. Try not to forget that you were one of us, once." She smiled at him, then stepped closer and gave him a hug.

Teeth had come into Bay City to pick some things out of his locker and had stopped by the swing room to say goodbye to his friends. Tom, who was still steaming from his early morning run-in with Whipcracker, and Ramon and Jimmy were in there as well as Marilee and Anita de la Cruz. Marilee gave him a hug and when Anita tried to shake his hand, Teeth grabbed her up in a big bear-hug. She rolled her eyes in mock embarrassment.

"Don't take any shit from anyone, Anita," he said while still holding her. He nuzzled her neck with a sloppy kiss, and she pushed him away. "And don't forget you're my girl."

"Get out of here," she said. "Go on—leave this sinking ship."

Teeth pulled himself up and puffed out his chest. "I repeat, I shall return." With that, he turned and left the swing room to exit the Bay City Post Office.

The others called out their farewells and told him they'd see him soon although Brian wondered how true that was. *I shall return? If you made it out of this post office, why would you ever want to come back?*

Marilee was giving Anita a quizzical look. She finally said, "You two were pretty close, huh?"

"Yeah, for a man he wasn't half bad." Tom was staring directly at her through the flat-topped black rimmed glasses in that owl-like expression that irritated her so much. "Oh, go fuck yourself," she said testily to him.

"What'd I say?" he asked in surprise.

"It's what you were thinking, Tom."

"Thinking?" asked Jessica. "Anita," she said in an instructional tone. "I believe you used 'Tom' and 'thinking' in the same sentence."

"Oh, right, Jessica," she conceded. "There is no scientific evidence that giant mobile turds have free thought. Not yet, anyway."

"What'd I say?" Tom asked again with his palms up. "Did I say anything?" he asked Jimmy.

Jimmy got up and pushed his hands toward the table. Before leaving the swing room he said, "Don't need no part of this shit."

Brian was laughing.

"Well," said Tom while getting up. "I do have a mind, you know." He ignored what Jessica was starting to say when he looked at Brian and added, "I feel so used when these two finish with me. Relieved, yes, but used. I hope I have something left for Earnie's blonde Swedish goddesses tonight." He walked out to continue dumping mail on the dock, and Brian laughed again.

"You should be so used, Brian," Jessica said causing Anita and Marilee to giggle. "And if you play your cards right..." She licked her lips suggestively.

Brian tugged at his collar as if to cool off, but he had to get up and leave before they noticed how embarrassed he really was. He couldn't figure out how she could get to him like she did, but she did. And there was always that glint of success in her eyes when she had finished torturing him with her flirtations. He moved quickly to the reg-cage and began making first notices on the C.O.D.s that had just arrived.

*****

It was seven-thirty the following night when Brian swung his Suzuki into Bill Rose's driveway in San Marcos. He saw Tom Short's old pickup truck with the camper on the back parked there, as well as several other cars, two of which belonged to Jimmy Winfield and Ramon Lopez. When he went inside, Tom was discussing in vulgar terms the two women he and the new man Earnie Franks had been out with the night before. Jessica West sat on the davenport alternately rolling her eyes and shaking her head. Brian sat on the vacant seat beside her.

"... and they couldn't get enough of us! This guy Earnie has a Jacuzzi on his patio, and we went in naked and did the old switcheroo right there. They both wanted to try the big guy." He tapped himself on the chest. "Damn! They were goddesses! And Earnie actually met them at the window! Damn! That Earnie's all right."

"Yeah, and tomorrow when your dick falls off, you'll find out why they was so available, too," said Jimmy.

"Earnie told them he used to be a free-lance gynecologist in Hollywood, and he checked them out first." Ramon and Jimmy started laughing.

"Brains, too?" said Jessica as she rolled her eyes again. "Sounds like your stereotypical whore. In your case, the perfect woman."

"They were beautiful. Full-bodied women with magnificent looks and of course exceptional taste."

"Taste?" asked Jessica. "Was last night an off night?"

"Arrgh!"

"Come on," said Bill. "Anybody would think you two were married."

"God forbid." said Tom.

"If there were no other humans on this planet, I could find a more appealing ape," Jessica responded quickly. Brian laughed. These two were continuing the verbal warfare they had initiated years ago, long before Brian knew either one of them. They carried it on regularly during working hours when they threw mail near each other.

"Let's get down to business," said Bill, and they all turned to him. "Everyone knows that extra pressure's on at work for some reason. Whipcracker, the Weasel, Diamond, and Phyllis Dunn have been conspiring to some uncertain end. And it's been making life miserable for all of us, some more than others," he said, glancing at Tom. "Their concerns aren't with production, but with vindictiveness, punitive retaliations, and plenty of other insensitive contravention of our rights, human and contractual. They know that they have Article Three supporting them, and that by the time the Union can get a fair resolution on a grievance issue they've created, the issue is long past."

"If we burned the mother-fuckers' houses down, we'd get a fair resolution," growled Tom.

"I can understand your personal feelings, Tom," Bill said. "I've got proof now, as if we needed it, that they're plotting to remove you from the service."

"Fuck 'em!"

"I know; but we've got to approach this in a rational way. For suggestions on ways to defend ourselves. That's why I originally called you all here. But now this other thing has come up, and it's even more revealing, possibly more damaging. When I said I had proof they were trying to remove you, Tom, it was no joke. Ramon, want to play the tape?"

Ramon set a portable tape recorder on the coffee table in front of him. He had transferred the miniature tape of his mail order voice activated tape recorder to a standard cassette at home, and now he plugged the cassette into the recorder to play it back. The first part of some words were clipped, but the familiar voices of Phyllis Dunn, supervisor of postal operations, supervisors Whipcracker, Darrell Diamond, and Lenny "the Weasel" Nicks, poured out. They listened as the conspiracy was laid out before them. None of the conspirators seemed to be the ring leader, but if rank has its privilege, Phyllis Dunn was most in charge, and she and Whipcracker were making the most damaging suggestions. They wanted everyone to come down hard on Tom Short without making any critical and obvious mistakes that could damage their case for his removal.

> *"Don't forget," continued Phyllis, "It will be ultimately our word against his. When we create a bad enough record of discipline against him, his union won't even want to support him."*

"Check the door," said
Diamond.

"I almost had him," said
Whipcracker. *"He was ready to
outright threaten me in front of
witnesses, but Rose and those other
asshole buddies of his came along."*

*"Well, if we work out a strong
enough case, he'll be gone in six
months."* Phyllis was wrapping it up.

"How about that Winfield?"
asked Weasel.

"Check the door," said Diamond
for the fifth time.

"Mutha-fucka!" Jimmy forced the words.

*"We don't touch that son-of-a-
bitch."* Phyllis's voice was adamant.
*"Jimmy's already cost us too much
money and embarrassment with
that minority crap."*

*"You mean he can do what he
wants?"* The Weasel sounded
incredulous.

"That's right, sucker."

"That's right, Leonard."

"Leonard!" Jimmy was laughing.

"Let me ask you something,"
said Whipcracker. *"Is he really still
seeing Sweet Sue?"*

The grunt sounded like the
Weasel.

*"You bet he is. Is she another
untouchable?"*

In the resultant silence, the mood in Bill's room grew suddenly
heavy. Brian looked out of the corner of his eyes at Tom who was
frozen in place.

*"Jesus!" said Diamond, breaking
the silence of the secret meeting.*
*"Let's not go there," said Phyllis.
"Not right now."*
*"When, then?" asked the Whip,
frustrated and unwilling to let it go.*
*"It could be fun," droned the
Weasel.*
*"No! It's too soon. Probably too
much at any time, now! Drop it."*
"Check the door."

Tom stewed silently throughout the session. When the tape was finished, he got up and said carefully, "I need to temporarily remove myself from the limited confines of your nice, particularly fragile home, Bill. But I'll be right back."

The others looked at each other and back at Tom as he ducked outside. His pompous tone meant trouble. In a moment Brian walked to the door and watched Tom's camper rock back and forth as the crashing sounds and muffled animal roars poured out of it into the crisp night air. All of Tom's recent frustrations and past delusions of persecution had become foregone conclusions in the space of a couple of minutes of tape. The noise subsided in the camper, it stopped rocking, and Tom stepped out with a quart bottle of Bacardi's rum in his hand. He looked up at the stars that were always brighter in the cold, shook his head, and tilted the bottle back. After several large chugs, he capped it and tossed it carelessly into the back of the camper where it clanked and rattled loudly as it landed. Tom slammed the door and came back inside. Brian followed him into the house. Jessica was talking.

"We all know this is incriminating as all hell. Let's give it to Whynaught."

"No way," said Ramon.

"We can't," said Bill. "We'd be committing a crime. This is illegally acquired evidence. Besides, do you think Whynaught would support us? He's about as big a liar as the rest of them, and he's got no backbone."

"Can we let the Blade have it?"

"Sure, if you want to let them print it with your signature as bona fide witnesses. You'll have to sign your name to the affidavit or they won't print it. And if you do, you're still liable for its illegal acquisition. Besides, how important would they think our little family dispute is?"

"Well then, what good is it?" Jessica was speaking everyone's obvious frustration.

Bill sighed. "For all practical purposes, it doesn't actually exist."

"And it's right there," said Brian. "Stripped as naked as the truth can be."

"I want a copy of that!" Tom pointed his finger.

"Sure, Tom," said Ramon. "I've got another copy. Keep this." Tom reached a huge hand down and tucked the tape away into a pocket of his corduroy shorts.

"Listen," said Brian. "We've often talked about putting a union paper together. Why not do an underground paper—no liability, but all the facts. And not just about this tape. About the conflicts, the personalities, the straight garbage we'd be legally responsible for otherwise. All the shit that goes on at work."

"I like that," Bill said. "You know what kinds of disadvantages we have while following contractual procedures—they speak, we listen. They accuse, we defend. It would be nice to force our facts on them for a change and let them answer to us. Yes! I like it."

Brian was surprised at how quickly and easily Bill had accepted the prohibited concept.

"That idea sounds great, as long as we put forward the effort," said Jessica. "I'm surprised at you, Brian, you bad boy."

"Not me," said Ramon, who, of course, knew something about everyone. "I was actually hoping you'd come up with something, Brian." He looked around at the others. "Remember that no one else can know anything about this," he said. "If we keep it all in this room, we'll be able to do it; I'm sure of it. We let it out though; we're up the Tijuana River without locomotion."

"He's right," said Brian. "We can have our own fun, and maybe even accomplish something by being a real thorn in their side with this, but only if we're discreet. If a single word leaks out, I'll deny everything." Everyone nodded agreement to that. "I want one other person in on it, a good friend of mine, a computer wizard, who can help us by laying it all out and printing it up. But that's it. No one else." Brian knew Charlie would never say a word.

"What do we call this rag?" asked Jimmy.

"Something to do with the truth," offered Jessica.

"OK," said Bill. "Ideas."

"The Naked Truth."

"Been used."

"The Plain Truth."

"Ditto."

"Who cares?" said Tom. "We're underground anyway, right?"

"Good point."

"Veritable Axioms."

"What?"

"Sorry," said Jimmy as he grinned. "Guess I'm still hooked to some of the shit I picked up during my EEO case. Believe me, management don't know what it means, anyway."

"I don't know what it means," said Jessica.

"Wow, and brains, too." Tom had slowly been coming out of his depression as the rum did its work on his mind.

"Well, have you got any ideas rattling around inside that Neanderthal skull?" she asked.

"How about Injun Joe's?"

"Injun Joe's?"

"Indians don't lie, do they?"

"Guess you never read Tom Sawyer?" Tom looked perplexed. "Injun Joe killed people and lied about it and nearly made another man hang for his crimes before he died in McDougal's cave." Jessica shook her head. So did everyone else—at her literary knowledge. She sighed deeply and finally said, "All right, Tom. It's the irony that counts."

"Perfect!" said Brian, and the others quickly agreed. He could see how pleased the decision made Tom and he was happy that

Tom had come up with the title considering his role in its conception.

They discussed ideas for articles, and they came up with several schemes that could become regular features if, as they expected, several issues of Injun Joe's were published. They would have a 'You Said It' filler of the best infamous quote of the week or month, a comic strip of the 'Weasel,' Jimmy's idea, something he said would really "piss off the little prick." It would also contain a contrived 'Postmaster Whynaught's State of the Post Office' message, and real hard facts concerning current issues of arbitrary discipline and actions against employees that seemed to take place for only vindictive purposes. They decided after some arguing to distribute the paper through the mail using untraceable funds to finance its operation. It would be dropped off into a remote collection box. Every carrier and clerk in Bay City would get a copy. The money would be redirected from the pizza and beer fund that covered gatherings after regular union meetings.

"Do you know how illegal all this shit is?" asked Jimmy.

"How legal is what they're doing?" asked Tom.

"That's why we've got to keep quiet about it," said Bill. "Tom, you must do everything you conceivably can to stay out of trouble on your own. Give it time, and the union will back you to the very end on what they're doing to you. I think that more than anything else, Injun Joe's will keep them off your back."

As they began to leave Bill Rose's house, Jessica called Brian over to her car.

"Pretty successful meeting, huh?"

"I hope so," said Brian. He nodded toward Bill's front door where Bill and Tom were still talking. "I hope Tom can hold it together. They're planning some real underhanded stuff to get him out."

"Say," Jessica started playing with the buttons on Brian's jacket. "How about a beer at Pappy's Pub?" The white tank top she wore under her leather jacket strained to contain her breasts.

Brian grabbed her hand. "Not tonight, you animal. I have a headache." Her actions no longer took him by surprise. Since he had known her, from the day he had started work here four years ago, she had always been extra affectionate toward him, treating him differently in a not too aggressive way than the way she treated anyone else at the post office. There were times when the thought of taking her up on her advances had entered his mind—she made an obvious and attractive offer—but so far he'd always succeeded in avoiding the perpetration of such thoughts. As it was, the playfulness assured him of his sexual appeal and gave him confidence in himself, especially welcome lately since Karen was so occupied off in her own busy world. But knowing that he was her only target also made her more and more difficult to turn down.

"One of these times I'll catch you in perfect health. Then watch out, honey." She pulled her hand free and put her finger to his mouth, and then she climbed into her little MG Midget. "See you tomorrow, Brian."

"Good night, Jessica."

Brian watched her back out and wave before roaring away in her little sports car. He climbed onto his bike, and during the cold ride home he thought alternately about how it would feel to make love with Jessica in a nice warm bed, and how the first issue of Injun Joe's would be received by fellow employees and the management at the Bay City Post Office. Both thoughts thrilled him, but Jessica dominated his thoughts with the assurance he could do with her what he wanted, without consequence, as long as he did it in his mind.

Chapter 4

"Police in El Paso appear to have found evidence to connect the deaths of two coeds in their city to those the FBI are now calling the Playboy Murders. The sexually tortured bodies of Cindy Hamilton and Kathy Brimstone, students at the University of Texas at El Paso, were discovered just off of Highway 10 near a rest area between El Paso and Las Cruces, New Mexico. Each woman had modeled for men's magazines within the past year.

"It is now believed that bodybuilder and ex-men's magazine photographer, Sterling Loudan, from Pensacola, Florida, is the Playboy Murderer. If so, Loudan is responsible for the murders of at least eleven women across the south, all of whom have posed at one time or another for various men's magazines. The gruesome string of deaths stretches from Florida to Nashville and now into Texas as he continues to evade capture, keeping a nation on edge. Police and FBI report they have intensified their nationwide search for Sterling Loudan, and they are now investigating reports of his possible ties to Southern California as they try to anticipate his next move.

"In other news today..."

Charlie Sharp snapped off the video cassette recording of Karen's news broadcast with the remote control.

"What a bastard!" said Brian. He was lounging in one of Charlie's overstuffed easy chairs in front of the TV.

"You've got it," said Karen. "A serial murderer out to destroy the objects of beauty that for some psychologically warped reason he finds detestable."

"Anyway, that's what I was talking about," said Charlie. He leaned up against Natalie on their brown leather couch.

"I hadn't even heard about this guy."

"One thing that I didn't mention on the newscast, Brian, is that he places the women in erotic poses where he dumps them. This guy is really sick."

"What are you doing recording my wife?"

"Are you kidding? You can look at her and ask me that?" Natalie punched him in the chest. "OK; Natalie records the news so she can watch it when she gets home. And why are women always hitting on me?"

"Don't try to make more out of it than it is, dear. Women hit you, not hit on you." Natalie said with a smile. "I don't feel like waiting until five o'clock to see the news after teaching two or three early English classes. Besides, Charlie's absolutely right, Karen—your newscast really is the best."

"Why, thank you. May I leave a card with my boss's name and number on it?"

"I think you two should be careful with that Playboy Murderer headed this way" Brian said. "He only seems to go after the beautiful women."

"Wow. Thank you. Are you going to be using him tonight, Karen?"

"I hope so," she said with a smile for Brian. "But, honey, we've never posed for a men's magazine."

"That's true, but what if he makes a mistake?"

"That brings up a good point," said Charlie. "He must have to case his women carefully to fit his sick profile. How the hell does he find the right ones, the ones who have posed in these magazines?" He raised his eyebrows at Brian. "Magazines I've never heard of."

Karen rolled her eyes.

"From what I understand, he does it in two ways," she said, sitting up on the arm of the heavy red leather chair. "One, he has a list of names and addresses of women across the country he has photographed in the past, and two, and most interesting, he sneaks into college gyms and while working out he inquires about women from the campus he's on whom he's looked at or read about in recent men's magazines."

"A lot of times the girls say in there exactly where they go to school." Charlie hesitated. "Uh, so I've heard."

"Why is he doing it?" asked Natalie ignoring him.

"Who knows for sure?" Karen shook her head. "It might have something to do with his ex-wife. I understand the FBI has her in protective custody. And I think she used to be a model."

"There sure are a lot of weird ones out there nowadays," said Brian.

"Speaking of weird, how's work going?" Charlie looked shocked. "God, did I ask that?"

Karen stood up and said to Natalie, "I think it's time for refreshments." She leaned over and kissed Brian. "And I think I've heard this soap before." She and Natalie went into the kitchen.

"We've got an idea for a newspaper we want to publish," said Brian.

"Secretly?"

"You're the only one, Charlie, outside of those who were at the meeting, and the girls," he tossed his head casually toward Karen and Natalie, "who will know about it."

"Time for some libelous writing, huh?"

"You've got it, big guy." Brian explained what was intended and how Charlie could help with his computer and printer in laying out and publishing the paper. He showed Charlie the notes he had written down concerning its format and subject matter. Natalie broke out some beer while Karen rolled a joint from the Sharp stash. Charlie had told the truth when he said, "She cannot cook, Brian. Period. But she can sure roll a clean number."

"Well, it looks like we can do it in about six pages. You're going to burn somebody's socks off with this shit. And I like the title, Injun Joe's."

"Tom Short's idea. He was real upset by that tape."

"You should use it. Give those guys a group name and transcribe the tape as an example of 'one of the blankety-blank Vindi-club's regular meetings.' They'd sure back off of Tom for a while."

"We're going to do it, and that's the plan. We hope that it does cause them to back off. As Tom would say, 'It is an underground newspaper, isn't it?' We just have to be careful about implicating Ramon, super spy. Someone will have to suspect a hidden recorder when we do that, and part of Ramon's cover might be blown. It would be sure to keep them on their toes, though."

"Well, I'm in. I'm tired of hearing all of the bullshit P.O. crap every damn time we go sailing. This way maybe you'll have some entertaining P.O. crap from time to time."

****

The next day at work, Brian walked in on the discussion of a big football game with the Carlsbad post office coming up in two Saturdays. Carlsbad had defeated the Bay City post office in both softball and bowling earlier in the year. Bill Rose was trying to find participants.

"Hell, yeah, I'll play," said Brian. "It's about time we beat those suckers at something. And it will take our minds off all the crap going on in here."

He punched in at the time clock and headed toward the cage to do C.O.D. second notices. From there he could participate in the discussion as the others threw mail.

"Well, you're our quarterback," said Bill as he stopped throwing to write it down. "I'll be center, Jimmy's our running back. Tom's our offensive line."

"Real funny, Rose!" came the resonant voice from the case behind Bill.

"Just kidding, Tom. You can share the line with Edwin Fernandez."

"I'm not running over Edwin's side," said Jimmy. "He cuts one of those Havana bombs loose and I get a whiff of it, let alone run full steam into it, you'll be carrying me off the field."

"I know what we can do," said Brian. "We can turn him around and have him fire one at their defense."

"God!" said Tom. "He'd wipe them out."

Edwin had been listening with amusement from his own throwing case, and now he lifted a leg and a low rumbling shook the floor.

"Oh, God!" said Tom. "He's let one go!"

"Break time." Bill headed for the swing room without hesitation.

Tom walked quickly to the drinking fountain as the nearly visible cloud floated toward Jimmy. Jimmy flew from his case as the first odor reached his nose.

"My gums is melting!" he hollered.

Edwin kept throwing mail and chuckling, apparently immune to his own deadly gas. It was hard to believe that such a little man could discharge that volume of caustic fumes and still have more left over; hard to believe until you watched him eat, or 'load-up,' as Tom would say. He could eat Tom under the table. The hotter, the spicier; the more corrosive the Latino food, the more satisfied Edwin was. And the little Cuban had been loading up the same way for the past forty four years.

Brian was laughing too hard to write. "Don't you know the Geneva Convention prohibits that sort of thing?" he finally said.

Tom was cautiously headed toward his case again. "They have a special section written up for Caribbean Cannonballs." That made Edwin laugh out loud.

Three women had been throwing letter mail in sit-down cases right outside of Brian's register case. They had been rolling their eyes and feigning disgust throughout the incident as they felt was appropriate for people of good standards and high moral character. Apparently the caustic fumes had not reached them.

"Honestly," said Marilee Willing. "I think that some people will never grow up."

"Obviously you're out of range," said Tom.

"If I have to put up with that all day, I'm taking sick leave," Anita de la Cruz warned. "I mean it."

Jessica smiled at Brian as she leaned over for him to see her through the separation in her case. "Do you think everyone's all right, Brian?" she asked.

"Fortunately we pulled through that one. But Edwin's like an earthquake—who knows when the next one's coming?"

"Edwin know," Edwin said from his case as he grinned.

"All right." Bill had snuck back to his case. "We need a couple of fast receivers to finish up the offense."

"How about Marilee?" suggested Anita.

"What do you mean?" Marilee asked cautiously.

"Well, we don't know what all you've caught; but we do know that you're fast."

Oohs! rang through the throwing cases.

"And you can play tight end," Marilee said haughtily.

More oohs.

"I want to play center, but only if Brian's playing quarterback," said Jessica as she leaned over to look at him again.

"You just want his hands on your ass any way you can get them," said Anita. Brian blushed and the others laughed.

"And you're just jealous of the quarterback," Marilee said to Anita.

"I'm playing center," said Bill before Anita had a chance to defend her lifestyle. "But we still need receivers."

Just then Earnie flew over to the water fountain. He stopped and looked at the girls on the way back. "Hi, Marilee."

"Hi, Earnie," Marilee said as she wriggled in her chair.

"Hi, Earnie," mimicked Anita as she exaggerated Marilee's movements.

"Oh, sit on it de la Cruz." Marilee frowned at her.

"I have, and I didn't like it."

"Well," said Earnie expansively. "I guess she's never sat on the right one, eh, Marilee?" With that, he flew back up to the front window.

"That's our wide receiver," said Bill. He wrote the name down. "He's slick, he's fast and I've heard he has good hands. I hadn't even thought about Earnie."

"Edwin!" Tom jumped out of his case just as Whipcracker came out of Phyllis Dunn's office.

"Hey! What is this? A party? Get back in your case, Short," Whipcracker snapped.

Tom growled, but cut through the air back into his case while holding his breath.

"Hey, bowse," called Jimmy. "Tom needs a han' wit his volume count." Brian hid his sudden smile as Whipcracker frowned and took his notebook over to Tom's case to measure the mail he was throwing. He tried to act nonchalant when the blast hit him, but the Whip's eyes were watering after he quickly made his count and left the case. Tom was still holding his breath.

"Sorry, boss," said Edwin with a sheepish grin. Whipcracker scowled and headed out onto the dock for some fresh air. He turned at the door.

"Two hours mandatory overtime for everyone."

"Thangs, bowse," hollered Jimmy. Whipcracker's face turned red, and he went outside.

Earnie came over to Brian from where he'd been listening up by the window while waiting on a customer.

"I thought I'd wait to ask," he said looking toward the dock. "No O.T. for you since you work so late, but now I'll be working until seven. Mind giving me a lift?"

Brian agreed and found out that Earnie lived only a few blocks from him in Encinitas.

It was early afternoon when the other clerks finished their overtime. Before everyone else started heading for home, Bill reminded them about the football game in two weeks. Brian and Earnie were discussing it when they headed out at seven.

"So, I'll be playing end, huh?" said Earnie. They stood by the motorcycle in the parking lot. A cool wind had come in from the ocean and was blowing through the darkness. Brian pulled on his helmet and gloves and swung his leg over the bike.

"You ever play football?" he asked as Earnie climbed on.

"Started three games at UCLA as a wide receiver," Earnie said. Brian wrestled to keep the bike up when he jerked around. "Yep. I got kicked off the team for cheating in English. You see, I'd been skipping the regular class but getting my grade by slipping into

Professor Susan LaBlanc's pants up in her little office. Somehow the dean found out, and I was off the team." He looked thoughtful. "I still think she was his little piece until I came along."

"That's a simple enough explanation," said Brian. He shook his head. "Did you do any good?"

"Well, she asked me back to her next semester class."

"No," said Brian. He started the bike. "I mean at football!"

"I caught four touchdown passes!" he shouted. Brian smiled, shook his head once more, and pulled away.

They took the coast highway toward home and stopped at The Leucadian for a beer. Karen was going to be late again tonight, working on several big stories including the Playboy Murders, so Brian was happy to go along with Earnie's suggestion to drop in at the bar for a few games of pool. Besides, it was fun getting to know this intriguing character. The bits and pieces he'd gathered since their first encounter at work had been encouraging, and Brian was discovering that he actually liked his electrically charged personality. It was when Brian brought up the Playboy Murders that he was introduced to the darker side of Earnie.

"Son-of-a-bitch!" he yelled, snaring the attention of several people in the bar. His jaw set hard, and he glared into the aura of light suffused onto the pool table. "You telling me the mother-fucker kills young, beautiful women?"

"Women who have appeared nude in different men's magazines. You haven't heard about him?"

"Naw, I've been settling in down here. Besides, I never watch the news. Damn!" Earnie looked like he was ready to break his pool cue against the wall. "If I had that son-of-a-bitch right here in my hands, I'd break his fucking neck!"

"Hey, take it easy, Earnie." He'd drawn the attention of a couple of women down at the bar.

"Why the hell can't they catch him? He's murdered twelve women, hasn't he?"

"Yeah, but the guy's a sneaky bastard."

"He must be some kind of fag," Earnie said while lining up his break-shot, "To kill beautiful women." His powerful shot bounced off the rack and ricocheted onto the next table where two Japanese men were shooting a game of eight ball. The two jumped when the ball smashed into the ones they were shooting. Earnie walked over and picked his ball out while they stared at him.

"I think you owe us a game," said the taller man. "Maybe you should calm down some."

"Calm down?" asked Earnie as he turned back toward them. "Twelve gorgeous women have been murdered by some fucking asshole, and all you're worried about is the fucking calm? In my America, women are sacred."

The two Japanese men bantered in quick singsong voices. Brian came over and said, "Let's get out of here."

"So!" said the short stocky one as he jumped into an exaggerated fighting stance in front of Earnie.

"What did you tell him?" asked Earnie, setting his cue stick against the table.

"That you one miserable asshole?" smiled the tall one.

"Where's your perspective?" Earnie hollered. He stuck a hand in his pocket and came out with a handful of coins that he tossed onto the table. Brian tugged at his arm while the entire bar watched the action. "Twelve beautiful women have been murdered, and all these two are worried about is thirty-five fucking cents. I almost forgot how these dickheads treat their women in Japan." He was pleading his case to the barroom. "Fucking assholes!"

"Assholes?" said the short one. He grabbed Earnie's other arm and jerked him around. Earnie's fist flew into the startled face, knocking him back against the pool table where he slumped to the floor. His tall friend jumped down to attend to him.

"Yes; assholes!"

"You in big trouble, sucker."

"Let's get out of here," said Brian.

Voices in the bar were already debating who was right or wrong when the bartender asked Earnie and Brian to leave.

"Twelve beautiful women!" Earnie hollered over his shoulder as Brian led him outside.

They drove back north up Old Highway 101. Brian pulled up to the beach and parked the bike. They hopped off and walked down near the ocean where Earnie pulled out a joint and lit it up.

"You carried that into work with you?"

"Yeah, I forgot it was in my pocket." Earnie shrugged and held it out.

"It's so much bullshit when someone says what they might do on pot," Earnie said. Brian took a hit, and Earnie went on. "I mean we've all been brainwashed by the idiots in Washington into believing that this stuff puts you out of control. Like I'm going to rape a teenager or rob a bank because my facilities for thought have been warped."

"They sounded warped back there at The Leucadian." Brian handed the joint back to Earnie after taking another deep hit.

"What the fuck's going on in this world?" Earnie asked. "Cigarette smoking has been found to be addictive—as if no one knew that before the Surgeon General gave us the official word—your trash can be searched without a warrant. Oh, Christ! Now what the hell am I going to do to get rid of my secret documents and the pounds of drugs I decide to dump?"

"And I thought you didn't keep up with the news."

"And now some shit-for-brains asshole is going across the country killing beautiful women."

"That's what's really getting to you, isn't it?"

He passed the joint back to Brian who took a deep toke, and he said, "The ocean's always had a tranquil effect on me." He looked out at the lights of a distant barge whose outline was defined by the starlit night. They passed the joint back and forth until it had burned down. Earnie flicked it into the ocean. They stood for a while with their hands shoved deep into their jacket pockets to keep them from the night chill as they listened to the waves breaking and crashing through the dark, rumbling up and down the shore.

"I don't always act that crazy, but twelve beautiful women. How sad."

"You're right, Earnie. It is."

Earnie looked at him and grinned. "You know, you're all right, Brian."

Brian gave a distracted nod. He turned toward the highway. "Let's get going."

"Yeah, I think I'm feeling much better, now.

"Hey, stud," he added, putting a hand on Brian's shoulder as they walked. "I've only been here a few days, but I've already seen a few things. You'd better take care of that Jessica West gal before she finds someone who will."

"She's good looking, isn't she? It's too bad I'm so happily married." He stepped over the bike and walked it backwards out of the sand. Earnie climbed on behind.

"Don't be a fool. I've seen how she acts around you. She treats everyone like low classed iguana shit until her stallion walks into the room. And she's not 'good looking'—she's fucking beautiful."

"I have a fucking beautiful wife," Brian said defensively. "And I don't think I need the headaches of an office affair. Who in their right mind would shit in their own backyard?"

"Then can I have her?"

Brian laughed and started the Suzuki up. They headed back down the highway toward Encinitas. Earnie shouted in his ear, "How fast can this thing go?" Brian opened it up a little, and in a flash they were doing eighty-five—more than fast enough, thought Brian, with someone on the back on this narrow stretch. They were slowing into the outskirts of Encinitas when the squad car pulled them over.

"Nice bike," said the officer as his partner flashed his light all around, especially into their eyes. He'd already pulled out his ticket pad.

"Thank you."

"You men been drinking?"

"We had a couple of drinks at the Leucadian, officer, ah, what's that name?... McGunther? Brian, here, said he could only have one. I had two."

"May I see your driver's license?"

"McGunther—I know I've heard that name before." Brian was fumbling for his license. Officer McGunther looked uneasily over a thoughtful Earnie and then back at his partner. "I know! Sandrella McGunther!"

"Sandrella? No! Thee Sandrella—her last name is McGunther?" asked the partner.

"Hell, Tim. Of course not."

"Are you related to my old friend?" asked Earnie. Brian held his license unconsciously in the air between himself and McGunther as he watched McGunther's perplexed features.

"Come here, son," he finally said to Earnie. He put his arm on Earnie's shoulder and steered him a short distance away, further narrowing the veiled secrecy defined by the range of their lowered voices. They exchanged their quiet words and Brian looked curiously at the equally puzzled Officer Tim. In a few minutes they watched as the two returned.

"Let's go, Tim."

"I don't understand."

"Later. Goodnight, gentlemen. I'd take it a little slower, now, Mr. McGraw, or that little woman of yours is going to have that little baby all by her lonesome."

"Baby...?"

"Later," said Earnie.

"Later," said McGunther to Officer Tim's inquisitive look. He imparted one more admonishment to drive carefully, and with a look at Earnie, who returned a conspiratorial wink, he climbed into the squad car and drove off.

Brian leaned up against his bike and looked at Earnie. Earnie watched the fading lights of the squad car.

"OK, now. What about this little baby? And who the hell is Sandrella?"

"Hey! You're asking me to impart confidential information here; to break a sacred trust with the Society of Men in Blue, our defenders of justice; to release maybe not so national but secrets never-the-less gained under fire and extreme duress..."

"Want to walk home?"

"Sure, I'll talk. I thought the baby part might add a little immediacy to our situation. And it'll keep Officer Tim off of McGunther's ass. What are they going to do, drive to your house and put their ears up to Karen's belly? They don't know you or her from Adam. What really got us off is the fact that I'm a close personal friend of Sandrella McGunther's. Hardly anyone knows her last name—I almost forgot it. She's the leading lady of the night life up in L.A. She's madam of two exclusive brothels. She's officer McGunther's sister. It must be a major embarrassment for him. Small world, eh?"

"His sister?" Brian was shocked. "How do you do it? You could be dumped into a vat of shit, and you'd still come up smelling like roses."

"Yeah, it's a curse. But in Sandrella's case, she knew my father. Real well." He gave Brian a curious sideways glance. "She's really a very sweet and worldly lady. I heard she came from a big family, but I didn't know she had a cop-brother. We do get lucky, huh?"

More to the dark secrets of Earnie, thought Brian. He pulled his gloves on and swung a leg over the bike.

"Yep," said Earnie. "Time to go."

They pulled away from the curb, and Earnie shouted into the cooling September night, "I need a woman!"

Chapter 5

"Short! Get out to the dock and dump some mail. Winfield! Take his place on the flats with Lopez and Rose." Whipcracker stood with his hands on his hips as he hollered out his orders.

"Yeah, bowse, since youse aksed so nice." Jimmy moved from the letters he was throwing to take Tom's place in the flat case. "Youse de betst bowse Ah ever did has."

"Knock off the bullshit, Winfield," Whipcracker snarled. "And get to work."

"Yeah, bowse."

Whipcracker shook his head and turned away.

"Hey, Whip."

"What?" Whipcracker growled, not even trying to disguise his irritation at the sound of Tom's voice.

"Where's my leave chit for next Thursday and Friday off? No one else was off those days when I submitted—I checked—so it's supposed to be approved and I think I'm supposed to have the approval today." Tom stood ominously in the middle of the aisle while the other clerks quietly worked and listened. Brian watched cautiously from the cage.

"Whoa!" said Whipcracker. A smirk had crossed his face. "You seem to know an awful lot about what's supposed to be."

"You got my chit?" Tom asked again.

"What chit?"

"I sort of expected that," said Tom. He reached into his pocket and unfolded the paper he pulled out. He held it up in a flourishing manner and showed it to the other clerks while stepping toward Whipcracker. "This is for next weekend, obviously presented in a timely manner and undeniably obvious to friendly witnesses." He slapped it into Whipcracker's hand and grinned.

Brian noticed that the Whip was still grinning, but he and Tom had expected that.

"Aw gee, Tom. Now it's too late. Your good buddy Brian is off along with another clerk next week on Thursday and Friday. And, hey, Lenny," he said as Weasel walked up. "On the clerk side, only two can be off at one time, right?"

"That's right," agreed Weasel with his perpetual scowl. "Your union agreed to that. Too bad."

"Oh hell," said Brian on cue. He walked over and handed Whipcracker a piece of paper after flourishing it the way Tom had. "I don't need those two days off. I'm relinquishing—in a timely manner—those two days.

"Hey!" he said. "That worked out pretty good for a change, didn't it, Weasel?"

"Don't call me Weasel."

Brian looked at him in surprise and walked back to the cage.

"See you lose that mother," Tom said. He tramped out to the dock to dump mail.

Whipcracker's joy had metamorphosed into a glowering displeasure, and he stormed into the office.

Weasel pushed his glasses up on his nose while staring at Brian.

"Real cute, McGraw. Got your hand in on another one, didn't you?"

"Don't know what you're talking about, Leonard," he said with a smirk. "Man just put in for some annual leave and got it approved. You can't possibly have a problem with that, can you?"

"Leonard!" said Jimmy with a laugh. "I think I'd rather be called Weasel," he whispered loudly to Ramon who also laughed.

Weasel's ears blushed pink, but he continued staring at Brian. "You're the one. You're really the one, aren't you? Always at the bottom of all the trouble. Just sneaking around in the dregs."

"Don't think so, Leonard," which caused another outburst from Jimmy. "If that were true, I'm sure I would have run into you a few more times than I have." Now Brian was staring back at Weasel with the same intensity.

"You guys are unbelievable. If you'd do your jobs right and shove your pitiful arrogance up where the sun don't shine, we'd all get along just fine." Jessica paused and then added, "It's only a lot to ask of a total asshole. Which of course you're not."

Weasel continued to stare, and then with an evil little curl of his mouth he said, "Sure," to Brian before turning on his heels and walking toward the carrier's section with that familiar hitch step.

"And stay on your own side!" said Jessica, not too loudly. "Why does that bastard always get involved with us? He's not our supervisor."

"Yes, but we love Leonard like one of our own," said Jimmy nodding seriously.

"Brings out that deep-seated cannibalistic *pasión* in all of us, eh, amigo?" said Ramon with a grin.

"That asshole's got a lock on you, doesn't he?" Jessica asked Brian. Brian was still staring after him although he was out of sight. "Brian, I'm talking to you."

"God, that guy gives me the creeps," he said. "I'd love to punch in that stone-cold evil rotten face."

"Brian, I love it when you talk rough. But we burned Whipcracker's ass, didn't we?"

"Got both them fuckers," said Jimmy.

"All that just to get the Animal his two days off," said Jessica. "Fucking unreal."

Brian looked through the cage at her.

"I'd apologize for my language, Brian, but it's the only one I speak."

"I was thinking that it is hard to believe that we have to go through so much to get so little."

Jessica lowered her voice. "That's not always the case, handsome."

Brian was startled for a moment before returning her smile.

"I'll remember that."

"Sounds like we're finally getting somewhere," she said while he left the cage for the front window.

Earnie was getting certified food stamps for a customer. When he handed them to the very heavy middle-aged woman in a long, faded dress, she stood at the counter and fumbled as she opened the letter.

"The bastards shorted me last month."

"You can open them over on a working counter while I wait on another customer," Earnie pointed out.

Her fingers continued their slow progress. She looked up and smiled while a few more customers came in to join the ever growing line. The next customer in line rolled his eyes and began loudly tapping his pencil on the shortened work ledge at the end of the rope divider that kept the customers in an organized line.

"I might need a witness."

"Ma'am, I can't witness anything," said Earnie. "I'm legally blind."

The woman looked up suspiciously. "Then where are your glasses?"

"Can't find them."

Her suspicions evaporated into a smile when he winked at her.

"Oh, you!" she said. She gathered up her food stamps and waddled away shaking her head.

The next customer was still scowling after her when he walked up to the counter.

"May I help you?"

"Yeah; two stamps."

Earnie issued the stamps and took the man's change.

"Thank you very much."

"Oh, and a money order for seventeen dollars and fifty-nine cents."

"OK," Earnie said slowly. His exasperation made Brian smile.

Earnie cut the money order and was turning back to the counter when the customer said, "Did I say fifty-nine cents?"

Earnie looked at him for a moment and finally asked, "How much did you want it for?"

"Seventeen dollars and sixty-nine cents."

Earnie sprung back into action and spoiled the money order. He cut a new one and said, "Will there be anything else?"

The customer looked at him with a hurt expression and said, "No, of course not." He paid Earnie, and as he was getting his change he handed back thirty cents and said, "Oh yeah; and an envelope, please."

Earnie slapped it on the counter while smiling a smile that didn't quite reach his eyes, and he said, "Thank you."

"One more thing," the customer said indignantly.

"What?"

"I'd like a consumer information card."

"You mean a complaint form? That's what *we* call it. Of course, sir. Take two. Here you go. Thank you, very much, sir. Next!"

The customer went to a work counter and started methodically and thoughtfully working on his consumer information card.

"Been a rough morning," Earnie said to Brian. "What are you smirking about?"

Brian closed Earnie's register collection drawer and stood up. Before he got out of earshot he heard an elderly lady say, "Young man. My money is stapled together so I won't misplace it. Will you help me get it apart?"

He laughed out loud when he heard Earnie say, "Of course your money's stapled together. Yes, ma'am, I'll help you."

Back in the cage, Brian listed the new registers and wrote up a few C.O.D.s for return. A short time later he carried an unclaimed C.O.D. parcel up front to put into the outgoing mail. The line had dwindled down and Maxwell, the other window clerk who would be retiring in less than a year, was waiting on the only customer. Earnie was chuckling over the consumer information card in his hands.

"I thought that he'd be complaining about me. That idiot is complaining about having to wait in line so long behind a fat lady; his words."

"You got some winners, today."

"Yeah, and about three other Columbo's, too. 'Ah, one more thing.'"

"You were nice to that lady getting food stamps."

Earnie chuckled. "You know, they come up to the counter with wadded up claim forms; they hand them to me along with their identification, both upside down, embarrassed to be picking them up. Yeah, I treat the people picking up their food stamps with the same, and maybe more, respect that I give to the guy buying five hundred dollars' worth of stamps. I just put myself in their shoes, Brian. Not only are they poor, being poor in this society is most of the time embarrassing. As if they didn't have enough weight on their shoulders.

"And I don't care how they got there, either. Some guys say they should get jobs. I say to them, fuck you. The jobs cost them money—they can't buy cars, or even keep up the clunkers that they can afford, and the babysitter takes a huge chunk of their pay if they do work. What a predicament. If they do get work for the sake of their own pride, they cut into the needs of their family.

"The least I can do is treat them with the respect they deserve, whether they know it or not."

"You've got a super attitude for the window, Earnie. I don't know how you guys up here do it. You face such a wild cross-section of the population and still maintain your sanity."

"Yes," said Earnie, crossing his eyes. "I'm sane all right. How about another ride home? We can stop down at the harbor for a beer."

"Sounds good. Karen's busy tonight—and all weekend, for that matter," he added with a frown. "And after another crazy week, we deserve a break."

Brian and Earnie pulled into Pappy's Pub at Bay City Harbor after work. It was Thursday, and they had mutually agreed that the great thirst that had overcome them was from their magnificent efforts of the week at work thus far, and drink as a reward was most definitely a part of their future.

"Hey, that's Tom's truck," Brian said. He pulled the Suzuki into a slot next to the truck.

"Let's buy him a beer."

"No violent Playboy Murderer shit tonight, huh?"

Earnie simulated a comic indecisiveness for a moment, and then said, "OK!"

Tom was sitting at the bar flirting with the woman bartender. He saw them, hollered hello and waved them over to a table near the open window.

"I've got our beer coming."

"I was going to order you one."

"You can get the next round. I owe you for getting me off next week.""

The bartender brought over three bottles of Chihuahua. Tom winked at her, and she smiled before going back to the bar.

"Things are pretty shitty at work, huh?" asked Earnie.

"You bet," said Tom. "Ask Brian—he works in the back, too. I think I need another night of hot-tubbing with those foreign chicks we were with." He looked like he was ready to drool. ""Blonde? Swedish goddesses?""

Earnie grinned. "They were nice, weren't they?"

"Made up for one fucked week." Tom took a big slug of beer and slammed his bottle down on the table. "You know, we've got to do something about those bastards!" Several heads turned toward them.

"Yeah, but what? Shoot 'em?"

"Now that's a great idea," said Tom, and an elfin smile spread across his face

Earnie glanced at Brian. "I understand you have a friend around here you've been visiting."

Tom stopped his bottle short of his lips. "Yeah?"

"Just wondering how serious it is, Tom. I'd hate to be leading you astray with my standards of living if you are spoken for."

Tom stared curiously at Earnie for a moment, but Earnie continued to stare back. Earnie had an extreme wild streak, but he had developed certain values he would not be swayed from. He leaned forward.

"If you have a serious girlfriend, Tom, the hot-tubbing with blonde, Swedish goddesses might be over."

"You dated a postmaster's wife."

"I didn't know she was married!"

Now Tom sat back, smiling and tilting his head. Earnie rolled his eyes.

"All right! Not everyone can look at relationships with the ease I do, OK? If you can live with yourself, fine. I'm just trying to look out for your emotional welfare."

"I can't figure you out, Earnie." He laughed and threw back a big swallow of beer. He looked around the barroom and then leaned conspiratorially toward them, but he wasn't smiling anymore. He looked at Brian.

"She's like a sister, and you know her. She used to work for the post office for a short time; eighty-eight friggin' days to be exact. Sue Brooks. Remember her?"

Brian thought for a moment, and then he nodded. "Sensitive young thing. She was there when I first started. Whipcracker used to..." He froze at the look on Tom's face. "There was a lot going on with her then, wasn't there? She didn't make probation."

"No, she didn't," Tom said. "That would have been ninety friggin' days."

"Was that who they were talking about on the tape?"

"They fuck with her again, they're dead."

"Geez, Tom."

"Who are we talking about?" said Earnie. He looked at both of them. "Now what the fuck did the Whip do?"

Brian went on. "He messed her over, didn't he? If everything is true..."

It is!" Tom interjected. "Every bit of it."

"Then what he did was criminal! Sexual harassment?" Tom nodded. "He couldn't have her—from what I've heard—so he got together with the others so she couldn't pass probation...?" Brian asked again.

"Yeah, the Weasel, that bitch Phyllis Dunn, that coward, Diamond. But it was mostly Whipcracker. Not much a sensitive young woman wrapped up in her own tragedies could do against that vindictive team of assholes."

Earnie was building steam as he shook his head in anger. "They ran her out of the PO just because Whipcracker couldn't force himself on her? Is that it? Come on!"

"Not only that; they wouldn't give her any time off when her husband left her," Brian said, remembering. "And she was an emotional wreck."

"What?" cried Earnie.

"Yeah," Brian continued, "I understand that the Whip drove her husband away because no one would step in and she was afraid to defend herself."

"She was only trying to make a good life for them, and they needed the money badly." Tom was trying to calmly explain it to Earnie, but it was clear he, too, was seething. "She thought everything would be taken care of after she passed probation. Maybe it would have been. She could get Whipcracker off her back, and her husband would come back. That's the only thing that kept her going through all the bullshit."

"And then he...," Brian paused. "She kind of went nuts, too, didn't she?"

"Not the best way to put it, but yeah, she couldn't make it. She blew up at Whipcracker one day, and he could see he would never get anywhere with her."

"I was there that day!"

"So they just let her go?" asked Earnie.

"Yeah, they just let her go. The lame motherfuckers drove her to try and kill herself. She only killed part of herself, though."

"Part of herself?" asked Earnie.

"Yeah; her head's still a little messed up; fragile. They keep her on some sort of constant suicide watch; doped up, too much, I think; but I still see a lot of good left in her. She just has to believe in herself. She's getting stronger. She lost a lot over all that crap."

"Geez," said Earnie. "How come she's such a secret?"

"Yeah," Brian added. "I didn't even know her well, and I never hear you talk about her."

"Because no one really cares. No one wants to hear about someone else's problems when they are facing their own damn problems. Hers could become theirs. People didn't care then, and they don't care now."

"Well I care!" said Earnie. "Now, anyway. People fucking with an innocent woman...! Shit!"

"This is why I don't trust the bastards—they still think she can come back at them. But apparently they found her."

"Maybe that's why all this shit is going on again," Earnie said.

"Why should they care about her? She wouldn't even hurt pieces of crap like them." Tom said. He held up a hand. "I don't think I want to talk about that garbage anymore."

"Maybe it's not her, but you they want to hurt."

"Seriously...," said Tom.

"Hold on a minute," Earnie said, ignoring Tom's plea. "So, she still lives around here?"

Tom rubbed his face. "She lives in a room at the Santa Margarita Hospital in Encinitas, Earnie. I visit her about two or three times a week; sometimes more often."

Earnie frowned at Brian. "A hospital?"

"It's an asylum...?" Brian said. "A..."

"A psychiatric hospital," Tom finished.

"No shit?" Earnie said. "They did that much damage to her? To a poor helpless young woman?" Earnie was getting very angry. "Why doesn't she press charges anyway?"

"Because they are fucking gold!" Tom slammed his fist down.

"Yeah, but if they drove her to that with sexual harassment—any kind of harassment; if those bastards..."

"I *don't* want to talk about it anymore!" Tom was clearly agitated, and they all took their cue, sitting back and drinking in silence for a few minutes. Earnie was steaming, and he and Brian let this new mystery percolate, and the many questions they still had dissipate.

"What are you doing this weekend?" Brian asked in an obvious effort to change the subject.

"Same thing I do almost every weekend." Tom took a deep breath, welcoming the redirection to something he would rather talk about. "I've got a place I go to, a Yaqui Indian village, southeast of Ensenada. The people there are my one true family."

Brian and Earnie looked at each other and back at Tom.

"I've heard that," Brian said.

"I kind of live there; and I help out when I can. It's my real home. Saturday I'm putting a roof on the new church. It's the icing on the cake for a long project we've been on. It's the end of four months of sporadic labor. If I get it done, I can play in the football game next Saturday."

Earnie looked shocked. "A church?"

His owl-like gaze met theirs. He shoved his glasses up the bridge of his nose and said, "I can sure use some help."

Brian broke the ensuing silence. "You're bullshitting, right?"

He smiled mysteriously and said, "Why don't you find out for yourselves? We can leave tomorrow night and be back by Sunday afternoon. I got a lot of work done during my last suspension."

Brian and Earnie were slowly getting past the disturbing revelations of Sue Brooks. And now as they looked at each other Earnie finally chuckled then started laughing. It was contagious and they all laughed. Finally he said, "You big son-of-a-bitch. You do have a family in Mexico. And I thought you were such a lonely boy."

"Nope, I have a big happy family. And they help me keep *my* sanity. These people don't need to surround themselves with lies and deceit—all they have to do is survive. I feel fortunate to be rooted in their lifestyle of hard work and honesty. You don't find much of that up here. Their world is a world of sanity. No one is trying to cut you down to their level or prove how much better than you they are with their superficial advantages or some staged, manipulative bullshit. No, it's not at all like it is here."

Tom got up and went to the bar.

"I've got this round!" Earnie hollered. He looked at Brian and said, "Can you believe it?" He glanced back at Tom. "I'm going with him. I won't believe it until I see it."

"I don't think I'll go. I've got some things to do."

"You're not sailing; you already told me Karen's working all weekend. So that's bullshit, Brian. Don't be an asshole—oh, I get it!" He nodded. "Hmm."

"What?"

"You're afraid, aren't you?"

"Afraid...?"

"You know; you want to know if the big guy really has a Yaqui village family and if he's really going to build a roof for their church, but you're afraid it's all true and you'd rather hear the disputable truth from me. That way you don't have to get too close to understanding how another cardboard person in your perfectly defined little world lives and breathes, and everything remains the same, unfolding just the way you always expect it should. After learning about his compassionate visits to Sue Brooks, this new church and family business with him must be cultural overload for you."

"What... what the heck are you talking about?"

"You're living in a box, Brian." He smiled and said, "Hey, you might like the peace you find there, and that disturbs you, too. You know damn well that you've got the weekend free. Come on! Let's go!"

Brian looked uncomfortable and knew that there really was no valid reason he could think of for not going. "I don't think 'afraid' is the word, but it all does seem eerie to me for some reason. What is he, their god?"

"If you don't go, I'm not going to tell you what happens there or how I feel when I get back. You'll never know." He leaned forward. "Come on. It's nice helping people."

Tom sat down with three more Chihuahuas. Brian finished his first one and set it in the middle of the table. He looked up at Tom and said, "We're curious, and, yeah, we want to see your village. Count us in."

*****

It was around midnight. They sat in lawn chairs pulled from the back of Tom's truck, drinking Coronas. They were on a small rise above the wedge-shaped valley they had driven up from. The moon was nearly full, and it showed off the tall palms bordering the road and the shadowy fields of grapes growing up the sides of the valley. They sat under a tall Eucalyptus tree on the edge of the Chief's little village, and the Eucalyptus aroma was strong and pleasant.

Tom told them that Chief Leyua was known as "*yo otai*, the elder spokesman," but Chief would serve just as nicely. The night noises were the rustling of the leaves in the gentle breeze, insects calling, a dog barking and then settling back down. Every now and then they heard murmurs of voices and soft laughter from the nearby shelters. Sounds of nature, of life.

"I told them I'd be staying outside with you guys tonight."

"What did the Chief have to say about us being here?" Earnie had his feet propped up on an overturned metal pail.

Tom's fingers were locked behind his head, and he had a Corona between his legs. He gazed over the valley.

"He told me to tell you thanks for coming. One of his daughters was going to bring us some food, and I told him it was too late, that we'd already eaten, but we'd be happy to accept the breakfast he offered for us in the morning."

Brian finished his Corona and set the bottle down in one of the three cases of Corona Tom had brought along. He stood up and stretched.

"I'm sleeping out here," he announced. "In my sleeping bag."

"I wouldn't do that," said Tom.

"Why not?"

"Rattlesnakes that like warm bodies, ants, scorpions. And we've got too much work to do tomorrow to lose you to some critter in the night. No doctors around these parts. Unless you want to submit to a little tribal medicine."

"Then I think I'll pass on that," Brian said, not knowing whether to believe him or not. "Thanks for the warning."

The truck was loaded with canned foods, blankets and toys for Tom's village, and tools for the church roof. He had planned a real celebration to go along with the work. Brian and Earnie rolled up in their sleeping bags on top of the camper, and Tom squeezed into the cab. He finally opened the driver's door to stretch out his long legs, and was soon snoring steadily.

Brian looked at the three nearby houses on his side of the truck. They were adobe, and heavy twilled mats of split cane stalks sat against the walls and on the roofs. The cane also made up a large part of the fencing that formed the household compounds. He wondered what it must be like to live under these conditions. Man is so much like a weed, he thought. He can grow anywhere, suffering only from his self-serving environment and the human-inflicted traumas he ends up forced to endure. But then again, some people seemed to prefer a more difficult and challenging lifestyle, back to nature and roughing it, living like those people who had no choice but loved their lives just the same.

Maybe going back was just something modern man did to convince himself that he was independent or still self-reliant. Or maybe it was just a crutch against the surrender of his original, but unattainable, high ideals or a defense against the dominance of some irresponsible power, and Brian thought of Tom and what Whip and Phyllis Dunn were doing to him and what they had done to Sue. That was so much another world. It was peaceful here.

He finally went to sleep contented in thinking about how doubtful it was that these people, these poor Mexican Indians, preferred to their seemingly harsh conditions the luxuries of running water, electricity, steady jobs, and paved roads to get them there on time.

*****

Brian rode his motorcycle down a winding dirt road past small adobe houses. Little Mexican children stood along the roadside staring blankly with big brown eyes, ignoring his cheerful waves. A white diaper-service panel truck was in his rear-view mirror. He thought it was unusual when he saw Karen sitting rather prim and proper on the passenger's side. He started to slow down until he saw to his horror that Whipcracker was driving behind the cracked windshield.

He opened the throttle but the bike coughed. "I've got to get rid of this fucking bike!"

Then he hit the soft dirt. He was on an incline, and the dirt swallowed his spinning back tire. He looked in his mirror and watched a jubilant, bouncing Whipcracker bearing down on him while Karen looked steadily on with accusation burning in her eyes.

"I'm sorry," he said. "I'm so sorry, Karen."

He was laying on the side of the road, now. An ambulance was coming. He sat up sharply when he heard the steady clang, clang, clang of the ancient Mexican ambulance.

"Who the fuck is he?"

Earnie was on his elbows staring across Tom's truck at a short white-haired old man who was grinning a toothless grin and bouncing an iron bar off of a stationary bell. The old man stood on the wooden porch of a low-lying building with his other hand clutching a colorful serape around his neck over a white cotton shirt and baggy white cotton pants.

It took a few seconds for Brian to separate his dream from the reality of the clanging bell. He rubbed his eyes and remembered the long drive and the many beers of the previous night. He looked at his watch. It was a few minutes past five.

"You all right?" asked Earnie.

"Yeah, sure."

The clanging stopped. Brian wriggled out of his sleeping bag and climbed off the camper. He quickly rounded up some warm clothes to throw on. Tom, impervious to the cold in his green tee-shirt and corduroy shorts, was stretching and yawning beside the cab.

"Food!" he said.

He led them into the building where the bell hung. It was the largest of about a dozen structures sitting in the middle of one of the large concave curves of the mountain behind the village. He shook hands and spoke with the little chief who grinned and shook hands with Brian and Earnie. The pleasant aroma of spiced Mexican food and warm coffee hit them when they crossed the threshold.

"Wow!" Earnie rubbed his hands together and marched to the long plank table that had been laid out with enchiladas, taquitos, frijoles, a soupy cornmeal dish that Tom called atole, tamales and fried bananas. He swung his leg over one of the long benches and sat looking expectantly at the chief.

When Brian and Tom had seated themselves, the chief motioned invitingly for them to dig in. He stood back with his arms crossed and watched with pleasure as the three devoured their breakfast feast. Two young, chubby women, shorter than the chief and wearing long white dresses with colorfully embroidered collars and sleeves and wearing their black hair in long braids tied off in leather strips, giggled as they served the hot coffee.

"Why don't they join us?" Earnie asked Tom.

"Oh, they'll eat when we're finished. We're the working men so they're giving us first go at this out of respect and because the chief says we'll need our strength." He looked up at the chief who was still grinning. "It's the most they can do for us, feeding us, and we should feel honored."

"*Sí*," said the chief, nodding his head.

"Does he understand us?" Earnie asked.

"Not one goddamned word of English," said Tom. "He'll understand how hard we work, though, and I'm anxious to get started. We've been working slowly on this church for four months, and now we're almost finished."

Light was beginning to filter over the hilltops and brighten the room where they sat. They ate mostly in silence, intent on finishing their meals and getting started. Brian hadn't seen the church site yet, or what materials they had to work with. But it was quiet, and it felt good knowing he was in a different place.

*****

When they'd finished eating, Tom led them around a corner of the village engulfing mountain. He stood in the middle of a wide, well-worn path and waited with his hands on his hips until they, too, came to a stop. Earnie let out a low whistle. They stood on the top, narrow edge of a valley that was separated from the valley they'd driven up late last night by a low ridge of hills. They could see both long, climbing valleys from their vantage point. On the left side of the ridge sat thirty or so adobe homes with green grass growing over some of the roofs. The twilled split cane mats were on nearly all of the homes. The homes were spread up to different levels of ground, into the mountain that still shadowed them in the clear morning air.

Women were already at work with the men harvesting in golden fields of corn and the brown and dark green fields of beans south of the village, and south of that goats and cattle grazed on the low, grassy fields. Twisted and thorny mesquites and dozens of tall palms bordered the widening valley as far down as they could see.

"I love to stop and look at all of this," Tom said. "Isn't it beautiful?"

"Beautiful!" Brian agreed.

"Look at that mountain," said Earnie.

Brian gazed at the rugged mountain with its perilously perched boulders and dark outcrops and then let his eyes wander over both valleys. "This alone was worth coming for."

"The valley with the grapes faces the ocean," Tom said. "It captures the unobstructed mist, even this far inland, from the sea-breezes, and that mist somehow helps the vines grow big healthy fruit for making wine.

"This is the valley," he said pointing back toward the homes leading into the mountain, "Where most everyone lives. Look at that little ridge of hills there. The stream flows into their valley from along the mountain and it gives them their surface water. It runs to a branch of the San Carlos River. Chief picked a good location, didn't he?"

A few of the Indians waved, and they waved back. When some children nearby saw Tom, they came running up. He crouched down and spoke to them in their language, and they listened quietly to him. In a minute, they went running away, laughing and chattering and waving back at him and his friends.

"I promised the *niños* toys tonight if they would help their parents."

Brian looked past the flat-topped, dark rimmed glasses and saw an unfamiliar sensitivity in Tom's eyes. He looked humbled and vulnerable in the wake of the children—actually at peace with himself—and Brian was shocked. There was love there. This sight was even more impressive to him than the sight of the magnificently divided valleys.

Tom stood frozen as he seemed to identify each individual of the village with a slow sweep of his eyes. After a moment he looked at Earnie and Brian and said, "Let's get to work."

Behind several homes and a hundred feet up the mountain was a level piece of ground where the thick-walled church had been started. It appeared to be wedged into one of the V's formed by the mountain that had blocked their view of this valley last night. A huge boulder, at least eight feet high, stuck out of the side of the mountain a few yards away from the church. About two feet of space existed beneath the mammoth obtrusion. Nearby sat Spanish tile, roof trusses, plywood and bags of cement.

Two little Yaqui men were dwarfed by Tom when they came up to talk with him. Their speech and gestures showed the friendly familiarity they all had for each other.

"They're going to help us," Tom said.

He led everyone to the pile of roof trusses and began carefully instructing in two languages. The two Indians took measurements and began cutting the overhangs of the rafters so they would line up with each other.

When Brian understood what they were doing, he grabbed a saw and began cutting. Soon they began handing the trusses up to Tom and Earnie who were stacking up top.

The long morning wore on, and around nine, when the air was warming up and the men were well into their work, the chief and his two daughters came around to the church. The daughters carried an earthenware jug of *horchata*, a rice drink that Brian found particularly refreshing.

When the daughters left, Tom invited the chief up to pound some nails. At first he declined until Tom said something that embarrassed him into going up. Brian had noticed that the chief didn't seem to do any physical work in this village. Tom laughed at the chief's indignity, but soon they were hammering away.

Ten minutes later, Tom slammed a finger with his hammer and said, "Aw, fuck!" He instinctively threw his hammer and added, "Shit," before sucking some blood from his finger. Brian watched the chief studying Tom with amusement and his eyes lighting up when Tom dropped down to get his hammer.

Soon after they had begun hammering away again, the chief hit his thumb with his hammer. He yelled out clearly, "Fuckshit!" and tossed his hammer through the air. It landed by the plywood and the roofing tiles on the ground. He grinned and looked at Tom.

"Why, you old son-of-a-bitch," Tom said. "We taught you English!"

When the chief went down to retrieve his hammer, he didn't return. Instead, he disappeared around the hills.

"That's the last we'll see of him while there's work to be done," Tom said. He laughed at something one of the Indians on the ground had said to the other.

"What did he say?" asked Brian.

"He said it was too late; that the chief had already destroyed the perfect image they had always held of him, and that the only thing that could save that image would be for him to send a daughter around to take his place."

Around noon, the daughters brought tamales, enchiladas and peaches out for lunch. Tom sent them for beers out of the cooler in his truck. Soon the workers were sitting back with satisfied appetites on rocks near the foot of the mountain admiring the view. After another fifteen minutes, they went back to work.

The work went faster, now, since the two Indians who had been cutting the wood below had finished the last cuts and come up to secure the S-shaped clay tiles. Two other Indians arrived from their own chores and helped load the tiles onto the roof, and Tom finished setting the last ridge tile into place just as the sun was settling on the horizon.

"We're finished!" he roared, and he repeated it in Yaqui to the delight of the villagers who had been slowly gathering in the evening to watch the final phase. He climbed down the wooden ladders with the others, all of them feeling like exhausted heroes.

Tom, Brian, and Earnie shook hands with the villagers and fellow workers while Tom exchanged pleasantries. He invited the villagers to his truck.

At the truck, Tom opened the camper shell and began distributing pots and pans, colorful blankets and field tools to the parents. He gave the families boxes of canned food. The children received dolls and toy trucks, and when he had finished, it appeared that no one had been left out. Tom got a big laugh when he offered a sturdy handled hoe to the chief. He innocently withdrew the gift as an honest mistake before offering the grinning chief a beautiful white blanket with a picture of a leopard on both sides.

When the villagers had gone to their homes, chattering over their new gifts, the chief had his daughters serve dinner to Tom and his friends while they sat out by the truck. Tom mentioned that they'd all been eating feasts compared to the normal meals of the village. The stars were bright and the moon was coming up. Tom thanked the daughters when they took the plates. And again Brian noticed the contentment in Tom that this little Yaqui village seemed to bring out.

"Where did you learn to speak their language?" he asked.

"My father used to drive a truck down here to haul off some of their harvested goods to Ensenada. He would bring back the items that Chief Leyua had asked him to pick up." Tom laughed. "The chief was younger then, but his reputation for laziness was already established."

"So your father taught you?"

"He taught me quite a bit, but the chief is the one who taught me the most—about the language and the culture." Tom sighed deeply. "I went with dad on his trips. Mom died when I was born, so it was just him and me.

"He took the chief to San Diego with him once while leaving me here in the village. I was six years old. When they got back, the chief was still all shook up by the loud and self-centered civilization he had encountered stateside. He talked my father into letting me stay in the village that whole summer. Chief told him I should have time to learn about peaceful coexistence with my fellow man and the earth that feeds us. Dad agreed, and for two wonderful summers I did that." Tom looked beyond the stars into a past only he could see. He took a big slug of beer and went on.

"Then one summer my father came down and took the chief into Ensenada. They were attacked by four knife-wielding Mexican bandits on the way back. They killed my father. The chief was wounded during the confrontation, but together dad and the chief managed to kill two of them. The other two got away."

Earnie and Brian were spellbound. Tom stared off into that painful past again after another swallow of Corona. An owl flew silently past the bright moon and dove sharply into the tall grass a hundred feet from them. It rose and flew triumphantly past with a mouse in its clutch while Tom watched. He took another drink of his beer and continued.

"I ended up in an orphanage in Chula Vista. I know what it's like to be alone."

Brian knew that was a reference to Sue Brooks.

"One night after my first week there, I snuck over the border and hitched rides until I got back to the village. The chief was proud of my great journey, but he told me I had to go back. He said it was important for me to grow up in the midst of my own culture— besides, the authorities and my own society would never permit this lifestyle, even as a guiding force, but he said it would always be here for me when I was capable of setting out on my own. He told me to have patience, and he called me his son.

"He took me back to the orphanage, and I didn't see him again for thirteen years. By then I'd finished school, served two tours in Vietnam, and started working for the post office. At first I started coming down here for his guidance on different things that bothered me, but eventually I realized that I was still accepted here as a member of this community. My spirit has never left. I found out that the villagers still celebrate what they call the death anniversary of my father. And now I have to come back, even if sometimes it is only in spirit—this is my home."

They sat in silence for a while, nursing their beers and absorbing Tom's story. It was a side of him that Brian had never known. All of this—the building of the church, the beauty of the valleys and the mountain, the revelation of Tom's past—Brian could see that its overall effect was not lost on Earnie, either. Brian had never seen him so silenced or introspective.

*****

Soon after that they all turned in, this time finding room inside the camper. In the morning they had another good breakfast and prepared to leave. Many of the villagers had gathered again, and the chief stepped forward to speak to Tom. He asked Tom to interpret what he was about to say.

"We have drifted far from the eight towns and the boundaries of the territory made sacred by the singing of angels, the *batnaataka*. But these are modern times and our families have expanded and overlapped in a co-parent, *kompai* relationship, a ritual kinship that most outsiders would naturally find complex and misunderstand."

The chief spoke in broad colorful words that were musical and foreign to Brian and Earnie, and he emphasized them with expressive arm movements while his eyes drifted across the canvas his hands were painting. His people were silent as they seemed to hang onto every word and every motion their *yo otai* presented. Brian finally realized why the chief was considered the elder spokesman by the villagers despite his aversion to physical labor— he was eloquent, knew the history, and knew how to associate it to the present.

"Our travel here has brought us Tom's father, and now Tom, my son, and for that this Yaqui village is grateful. He is *wawain*, kinfolk, and he is godfather to many children of our village. It is an honor we do not hold lightly.

"And him we thank for bringing you to us. You we thank. Our village will remember your help in every forthcoming ceremony. The roof you built is strong and durable and capable of housing our faith, keeping us strong, and 'joined,' even at this distance, to the sacred tribal territory. Thank you Brian and Earnie. Come back to us soon."

The chief's 'Brian' came out 'Bry-ee-an', and 'Earnie' was close and followed by a huge toothless grin. He shook hands with all of them, and the villagers who had gathered followed suit.

Soon after they hit the road feeling the soreness in their muscles but relaxed in the aura of their good work and the friendliness of Tom's village. Earnie sat in the middle while Tom drove down the valley of grapes and onto another dirt road leading to the highway between Ensenada and Tijuana. This was mostly desert, with much cactus, a few mesquites, and an ocean of sand and rock. Brian hung his elbow out the window to make room for the good-sized to huge bodies in the cab. The warm air circulated through the truck and left him in a dreamlike state. Everything was so open here—no buildings and no people. He was more than agreeable to the joint Earnie pulled out of his shirt and fired up. He was even more surprised by Tom's reaction.

"Get that thing out of my truck!" he hollered. When Earnie hesitated, Tom reached over and snatched it away. He flung it out the window and asked, "You got any more of that shit?"

Brian was stunned, but Earnie seemed to retain his composure.

"Uh, by the way, do you mind if I smoke?" he asked casually.

"Yeah, I mind, damn it Earnie. Why didn't you tell me you had that?"

"Gee, I guess I didn't realize how important it was to you, Wally."

"Do you have any more of that shit on you?"

This time Tom looked incensed, and Earnie took the cue.

"No! Geez, Tom. What's wrong with you?"

"Are you sure?"

"Yes, damn it! Now what's going on?"

"I hate that shit."

It was too simple of an explanation. Brian was curious too, and he and Earnie stared at the giant peering out of the windshield attempting to concentrate on the bumpy dirt road. Brian realized for the first time that he had never seen Tom smoke a joint.

"OK!" Tom said. He glanced at the two of them, then back at the road. "Remember those four Mexican assholes who jumped my dad and the chief when they were coming back from Ensenada? They were fucked up on weed. The chief told me that the odor permeated the air, that one of the guys had a joint hanging out of his mouth and offered it to my dad before they pulled out their knifes to rob them. It's bullshit! Some of the villagers smoke it, but I refuse to set a bad example for all those little kids. When I was in Vietnam some of the biggest idiots in my unit almost got us all killed by getting fucked up on weed when they were supposed to be on duty—some of those dumb-fucks got themselves blown away because they reacted too slowly."

"Yeah, that was stupid," agreed Earnie. "But where are the Viet Cong around here?" He spread his hands out taking in the desert.

"They got his father, Earnie."

Earnie thought about it for a moment, and they were all silent.

"I'm sorry, Tom," Earnie said. He shrugged. "You surprised me, though. I thought a big partying guy like you would enjoy a little weed now and then. Sorry I brought it up."

Tom slapped a huge hand on Earnie's knee and said, "It's no biggy. I just don't want it in my truck or my house or so close to my people if I can help it. And besides, I don't want it around me when I'm crossing the border. Those fuckers would be glad to rip off my truck for a joint of marijuana. It's illegal, you know. Why do you smoke it?"

Brian spoke up. "I thought you said something about civil disobedience and moral rebellion once."

Tom gave a start and before he could speak he laughed. Earnie gave Brian a curious look.

"OK, OK! You've got me there. What you do is your own business and how you go about it, the same. I guess the bottom line is I don't like that shit. I guess there might be a time and a place for it—everybody's not always fighting wars or defending themselves from sociopathic assholes—and I guess if you want it legalized you have to push your point. Moral rebellion and civil disobedience. Man, you got me there, Brian." He laughed again then said, "Just keep it away from me."

He looked back out the window and concentrated on the road.

Brian stared out the windshield for a few moments, then at Tom and back to Earnie. He finally said, "This sure has been a change of pace from weekend sailing."

Chapter 6

The Saturday morning sunlight poured over Brian's right shoulder. He glanced at the sky. A gentle but steady Santa Anna wind was clearing away any trace of clouds and was quickly warming up the day as it blew in off the desert.

One of the mildest weeks in memory had passed with Whipcracker on vacation and Phyllis Dunn on assignment in San Diego. Lou Lambier, a carrier who was working on becoming a supervisor, was a communicating and understanding temporary replacement for the Whip. Tom Short had taken his two days of annual leave with little fanfare and no resistance, and the talk of the week had centered on the upcoming football game against Carlsbad.

It would be hot by the time the football game began, hot for the first time in several weeks. Right now he was riding into work to show Bill Rose a copy of the Injun Joe's newsletter he and Charlie had finally finished and mailed out, and to invite Earnie to Donnie Bonito's party aboard the Columbo after the game.

Brian looked in his left mirror and saw a red 280Z approaching quickly in the fast lane to his immediate left. Traffic was unusually light. Suddenly he saw a police car on the 280's tail approaching even faster. When the speeding car came up next to him, the young girl who was driving applied her brakes and slowed rapidly. The police car's brakes were slammed on, and when it nearly hit the Z, the officer driving began to swing into Brian's lane. Brian swerved, just missing the police car's back fender. The officer got control and looked apologetically and sheepishly at Brian who at first frowned and then gave a smile of resignation as he pressed on.

"I am invisible," he mumbled while looking in the mirror at the two cars that had finally pulled over.

"Hey, Bill," called Brian. He walked into the swing room where Bill, Jessica West and several others were eating their lunch. They had come into work at 2:30 a.m. and would be off at eleven. Lunch came early under those conditions.

"What have you got there?" asked Bill.

Brian handed him the newsletter, and Bill opened it just enough to see what it was before slipping it, folded, into his back pocket.

"I'm going to be at the game at one in case you need me." Jessica smiled. She stood up and stretched her arms over her head, and the men eating their lunch, talking or reading the newspapers, all paused in whatever they were doing to watch the impressive sight. She walked around the table and brushed past Brian stopping with her body against his just long enough to whisper, "See ya at one."

Earnie had just come into the swing room when Jessica began her show, and he winked crudely at Brian. Brian could feel his face burning as he watched her walk out.

"Wow! I'm impressed," said Earnie.

"Hey, Brian, aren't you happily married?" asked Bill.

"So are you," said Brian.

"Not so happily. I could be happier." He shook his head as he looked out the door.

"Ah, wouldn't you know it," said Earnie. "A perfect marriage fucks up everything." Brian winced. "To tell you the truth, though, I think you ought to stop beating around the bush. There's no way a man can resist such temptation. Might as well get started on it."

"I think she's started on it enough for the both of them." Bill scratched his chin and looked back out the door.

"Come on you guys. She's just teasing; playing some kind of game."

"Cut the shit, Brian. She's a beautiful woman obsessed with fucking your brains out, and we all know it. Anytime, anywhere, anyhow."

"Aw; don't go there again, Earnie. That's disgusting," he said looking around. "Thank God there are no women in here."

And over Brian's objections, Earnie went on, "Forget about archaic moralities, fool. This is the twentieth century, the 1980's, a step beyond the free love era, more sophisticated than that. Man is living longer than marriage vows were originally intended to last. Only eunuchs and popes could survive such insular antiquated conviction in a day of hard bodies in string bikinis, black, low-riding lace panties, Dr. Ruth and Jessica West.

"Besides, can you imagine her naked?"

Someone in the swing room whistled.

"Look at it this way—you owe it to mankind to take her out, rip her clothes off and fuck her silly." Brian put a hand to his face while the guys grunted agreement, encouraging Earnie as he went on. "Not for yourself; not just for her. But for Abe Lincoln, John Kennedy, Jimmy, here, and for your children's children. Ravage her, son. Take the monkey and run; the fuck stops here. Do it for yourself—do it for her—hell, do it for me; but for god's sake, do it for mankind."

Earnie mocked weariness as he sat in the chair offered by Bill Rose while the others clapped their hands.

"That's all I have to say. The rest is up to you."

"That is so vulgar I can't believe I just heard it," Brian sniffed. "I won't justify that with a comment to any of you guys."

"Perfect," said Earnie. "Keep it discreet."

"I've got to get out of here," said Brian, rolling his eyes. He got up to leave while they laughed, and then he turned back around. "Don't forget, we've got a big game today. Try and get your perverted minds out of the gutter and onto the playing field. Right, coach?"

"Not to change the subject," Bill said with a grin. "But that's right. Carlsbad still has all the bragging rights from the softball game and our bowling match last summer. I've told everyone to try and get there at about twelve-thirty so we can go over a few plays. Earnie will be a little late since it takes a half hour to close out after the Saturday window shuts down at noon."

"All right," said Earnie. "Let's kick some ass today." He saw Brian motion with his head and followed him out the door. They walked out onto the back dock.

"I see you have to work today."

"Just until noon, or so," Earnie said. "A little overtime won't kill me. I can use the money. That piece of shit I'm driving is falling apart. So, what's up?"

"We've got room for two more on Donnie Bonito's sailboat for the party later this afternoon. Want to come?"

"Heck yeah!" He paused. "Can I bring Marilee Willing? I'd like to find out how she got her name."

"That's fine with me. Charlie and Natalie, Donnie and a few friends from the studio and of course Karen will all be there. We'll have lots of room. It's a huge forty-nine footer."

"Thanks for the invite, Brian." He slapped Brian on the shoulder. "And don't worry about the game. The second-best thing I do is catch a football." He turned and ran back into the building.

Brian watched until Earnie was out of sight around a row of throwing cases. He stepped off the dock and hopped onto his motorcycle. There was something indefinably magnetic about Earnie. He was crude, arrogant, and cocky, but he was also sensitive and understanding when he wasn't on stage, and when someone needed those feelings from him. Brian liked being around him enough to invite him to a party that even he might feel out of place at. But he knew Earnie would fit right in. Maybe his unpredictable nature was his attraction.

They'd known each other only a few weeks now since Brian had threatened to kick his ass "from here to the Bay City Pier," but Earnie's intriguing personality had since overcome their inauspicious introduction. Brian shuddered to think of it, but he found a lot of his own underlying personality, although more subdued, in that loud, mysterious and maybe even crazy character from L.A.

I wonder if he can really catch a football? Brian thought. He started up his bike and kicked it into gear.

*****

In the afternoon the light breeze had picked up and given way to a strong breeze, conveying a penetrating warmth on its wings. The unobstructed sun beat a steady unselfish rhythm of heat on the arms and shoulders of the athletes preparing for their contest. The field at Jefferson Junior High School was in beautiful condition, and some joggers from the cinder track surrounding the field found comfort in the softest spots on the edges to sit and relax and watch the warm ups.

"Just pass me the got-damn bawl!"

"Where's Earnie?"

"If he don't show up soon, we in some deep shit." Jimmy pleaded with Brian, "Now, pass me the bawl, huh?"

Brian fired the ball high and it bounced out of Jimmy's hands. When he went after it, one of the Carlsbad players picked it off the turf and underhanded a shot that buried itself in Jimmy's midsection. He held the ball against his stomach with one hand and winced a "thanks" with a wave of his other. He walked painfully back to Brian.

"I know who they quarterback is."

Bill Rose jogged over from where he'd been talking with the Carlsbad team captain. He handed Brian and Jimmy yellow belts with two dangling yellow strips that were hooked to the belts with Velcro.

"Put these on. They're kicking off to us first. Where's your buddy Earnie?"

Great; now he's my buddy, thought Brian. "Wish I knew. Maybe he had to work a little more overtime."

"We've only got six guys, and they insist on playing seven on seven." Bill looked over at Jessica. She was turning cartwheels on the sidelines in front of Ramon, Tom and Edwin Fernandez who were as entranced as Anita de la Cruz by the flashes of orange panties under the white skirt. "Hey, Jessica!"

"What?" She stood with her arms in the air and her legs apart after finishing her athletic display. Tom started hooting and clapping his hands. "Dry up, mutton-head." She jogged over to Bill with Ramon, Edwin, and Tom on her heels.

"Let's play ball," said Tom.

"We can get started if Jessica is willing to play for a while," said Bill.

"Wonderful," muttered Brian.

"What's that, sweetheart?" Jessica stepped close to Brian with her hands on her hips, thrusting her ample chest against his. "I think I can handle anything you throw my way." He grinned sheepishly and felt his face out heating the pounding sun. She turned and faced Bill.

"Sure; I'll play."

Tom and Jimmy yahooed and threw their fists into the air. They all headed for their positions and Bill hollered to the Carlsbad team, "Let's do it!" He positioned Jessica after discreetly advising her to just try and get in the way but not get hurt.

Jimmy took the end over end kick-off near his own goal line and headed up field. He gained yardage to the halfway line in the shortened field with fancy footwork and quick spins before being unceremoniously shoved out of the sidelines by two burly Carlsbad players.

"Hey, just pull the flags, huh?" yelled Bill as Jimmy picked himself up and headed for the huddle. "You all right?"

"Shit, man," he said, brushing off some grass. "They's some big fuckers."

According to their predetermined rules, they had six plays to either score a touchdown or turn the ball over to Carlsbad. After five they had gained half the remaining distance on a single reception by Jimmy.

"We could punt into a corner," said Bill. "I wish I knew where the hell Earnie was."

"Or you could pass the goddamn ball to me!" Jessica was glaring at Brian, who along with the others had turned to stare at her with surprise. "Well, I've been open," she said a little sweeter.

"What's this?" asked Tom. "Trouble in paradise?"

"I just want to be part of the team. My position isn't 'left out,' is it? I'm sorry, Brian, but if you don't need me, I'll just watch the game with Anita on the sidelines."

"Of course I need you, Jessica." He added quickly, "I mean we need you." Her smile nearly melted him. "Don't we, Bill?"

"Great line," offered Tom. "Saved your ass and got this bitch in heat."

"Stow it, knucklehead," said Jessica. She continued to smile at Brian and caught him off guard with her next question. "Why wasn't I invited to your party?"

"Hey! Let's play ball, you guys!" hollered a Carlsbad player.

"OK," said Bill. "Jessica, get open in the end zone on the left side; and Brian, hit her with the pass."

"See if you can catch this one as well as you did the one in the huddle," said Tom. He scrambled to his blocking position while the others laughed and before she could contribute a response.

Bill snapped the ball to Brian who faded back, looking in the direction of his normal primary receiver, Jimmy. Suddenly he turned and fired the ball deep into the left corner of the end zone. Jessica stood with her arms open, and when the ball hit her in the chest, her hands came down around it. She fell backwards with her dress flying up around her waist. The late arriving Carlsbad defender slipped trying to knock the pass away, and he fell with his face ending up in her crotch while her dress settled over his head.

"Get the hell out of here, you fucking pervert!" she yelled. She pushed the grinning face away. The rest of her team came running up laughing and cheering.

"All right—our secret weapon," said Bill.

"With a weapon like that, why keep it secret?" Tom asked, looking at her with open hunger.

"No wonder you're such an idiot," said Jessica standing up and straightening out her hair and clothes. "Your brain cell is getting lonely."

On the ensuing kick-off, Jimmy caught the Carlsbad receiver and grabbed both flags. He hung on and leaned backwards with both heels sliding along the grass.

"Hey! Those flags are sewed on!" yelled Ramon.

Tom caught the runner, with Jimmy in tow, and tackled him to the ground. He ripped the entire belt off the shocked player and stood over him holding it up like a prize scalp.

"Arrgh!"

"What the hell are you guys doing?" Bill Rose was screaming in the face of the Carlsbad captain. Players were standing around shouting at each other. Eventually the two captains agreed to a ten-yard penalty from the point of contact—"It was just a joke," said the other captain—and play was resumed.

At one-thirty a ten minute halftime was called. Carlsbad's quickness had put them in front fourteen to seven despite the heroics of Edwin Fernandez who had thus far laid two low-level air-eaters from his offensively defensive end position, stopping the respective runners for a loss, but also holding up the game on each occasion.

They sat around on the grass more to catch their breath than to plan strategy. Jimmy had caught a few more passes, but it was evident now that Jessica's touchdown reception had been a fluke. She wasn't even insisting that Brian pass to her anymore.

While they rested, a black limousine pulled up along the other side of the fence just past the south side of the cinder track. A pretty blonde haired chauffeur wearing a black hat, a white shirt with black bow tie and black slacks stepped out and opened up the back door. Earnie and Marilee emerged and waved to the group. They came through the gate and walked over hand in hand. Brian saw the look of chagrin on Anita de la Cruz's face as she half-heartedly returned Marilee's friendly wave.

"Hey, guys! What's the score?"

"Where have you been?" asked Brian.

"I asked Marilee if she could come to your party with me, and she and I took a slow ride in the limo while she made up her mind." He put his arm around Marilee and gave her a gentle squeeze. "She said yes."

"Well, I'm glad you're here," said Jessica. "You can take my place." She looked at Brian. "Even if I'm not invited to the party."

"What's with the fancy wheels?" asked Jimmy.

"I figured that if I'm taking a beautiful woman to an exotic ship party, then I might as well go in style."

"You mean you've got that limo all day?" asked Brian.

"And all night," said Earnie with a wink for Marilee.

"God, let's go sit down," said Jessica. She took the arm of the enchanted Marilee and walked her to the sidelines where Anita sat fuming.

"Now tell me what the score is."

"Fourteen to seven," said Bill. "And I think it's time to start the second half."

They picked themselves up, and after positioning Earnie, they kicked off.

*****

After five of the six plays that Carlsbad had to score, they were still deep in their own territory forcing them to punt. Brian saw that Earnie had good athletic ability, and even though he hadn't handled the ball yet, he had made good defensive moves in knocking down two passes.

"OK," said Brian. "We've got a rested player; let's hit him with the bomb."

"Sí, bueno!"

"No, not you, Edwin!"

"Heaven forbid," said Tom. "Keep the plug in."

"What we're going to do is let Earnie fly."

They broke the huddle and lined up. There was some confusion on Carlsbad as to who would cover the new man. On the snap, Earnie flew past his defender, and a moment later Brian set sail with a deep pass. Earnie glided under the football and deftly pulled it in. Without breaking stride, he swept into the end zone.

"That's one!" he hollered. Jessica, Marilee and Anita cheered on the sidelines and his teammates ran up to congratulate him.

"Nice catch," said Brian.

"Nice wheels," said Jimmy.

"Well, let's get some more," said Earnie. He tossed the football to Tom for the kickoff. "This might be fun."

*****

For the next half hour, Brian watched his team's efforts double in an effort to keep up with Earnie. Everyone was playing over his head. Even Edwin intercepted a pass on the last play of the game, although stopping him nearly proved tragic for Carlsbad. Edwin had tripped when the player reached for his flag, and they both fell. With one of his better efforts, Edwin unloaded a shot that lifted his tackler three feet into the air. The Carlsbad player landed hard, but it was a couple of minutes before the air cleared enough, even in the stiff warm breeze, for anyone to assist him. His first words were, "Oxygen! Oxygen!" With the score at thirty-five to fourteen, that proved to be the final play of the game.

Carlsbad players shook hands with the celebrating Bay City players before heading off to nurse their wounds.

"We finally got them," said Brian.

"Yeah, but they'll be back," said Bill in somber tones. Then he shouted, "But until then, we've got the bragging rights!"

Earnie whistled and signaled to his lovely chauffeur. She brought over four bottles of champagne in a bucket of ice. Tom salivated, his eyes bouncing from her to the champagne and back to her.

As they drank and reenacted the game, Brian watched Jessica. She wasn't enjoying the celebration as much as the others, although her touchdown was the topic of much discussion. He walked over and sat down beside her. He offered her a drink, and she tipped the bottle up. Why the hell not? He made up his mind.

"Jessica, I'm sorry I didn't ask you sooner. But would you like to come to the party? Some friends of mine and Karen's will be there, and Earnie and Marilee. We'll have lots of room..."

Jessica's eyes brightened, and before he could finish, she wrapped her arms around him letting the bottle fall to the ground. She gave him a passionate kiss.

Brian was barely aware that the conversation had stopped around them.

"I've got to go hurry and change," she said when their mouths separated. She held his face in her hands and lightly kissed his nose. "I knew you would invite me, Brian." She jumped up and jogged across the field to her car. He finally turned his gaze back to the stunned faces, dreading what would be said.

"Why, you sly dog," Earnie said, toweling the sweat from his face. "Maybe my speech in the swing room didn't go to waste."

"My, my," said Anita. "I'd sure like to hear what Karen thinks of your little heartthrob. She must be very open-minded about such things."

"Wish I was going to that party." Tom stared owl-like at Brian.

"There's no more room on the boat."

*****

The wind had finally begun to settle down, though the heat pervaded. The late afternoon onshore drift of air created a near stalemate with the desert wind. Many of the boats in the Bay City harbor were occupied by the relaxing owners and their guests, and they were enjoying this most recent tail-end of summer. Shorts and bikinis adorned the summer-browned majority of the harbor community.

Brian and Karen arrived in vogue, dressed to enjoy these last few hours of sunlight. They drove from Encinitas with the top down on Karen's Rabbit.

Brian had rushed home on his motorcycle after the game and found Karen trying on different bikinis in front of the bedroom closet wall mirror. What followed resulted in clothes strewn all over the bedroom and a randy twenty minute delay in getting to Donnie Bonito's party. It was three-thirty, and the sunning rays were vanishing, but they still had nearly three more hours of daylight left in which to soak up the heat on their bare skin.

The whole gang was already there. Donnie welcomed them aboard, and Brian introduced Karen to Earnie who had already charmed his way aboard.

"Permission to come aboard?"

"Who goes there?"

"Guests of Karen and Brian McGraw, Mr. Earnest Franks and Miss Marilee Willing. If the captain would permit us aboard his yacht, we would be honored."

Jessica had also arrived, and she ducked under the boom and made her way over.

"You must be Karen," she said holding out her hand and smiling. "I'm Jessica West. Brian and I work together."

As she shook hands with Karen, Brian tried to keep his gaze from her magnificent body. The orange bikini she wore looked as if it had been painted onto her tanned flesh.

"Brian hasn't mentioned much about you." She looked at him for a moment and then back at Jessica. "But then, I can see why not." She smiled and said, "I'm very glad to meet you Jessica. Let me show you around the boat." They left him standing red-faced and maneuvered their way below deck.

"Wow, nice party." Earnie had been ogling the two as they walked away. "Here—have some champagne. You look like you could use a drink."

Brian took a big swallow and said, "I'm glad I invited her." He slowly shook his head and whistled.

"I am more envious right now than I have ever been in my life." Earnie laughed. "You son-of-a-bitch! We're even more alike than I thought."

"Hey, don't be making a big deal out of nothing."

"Nothing? Don't tell me again that you haven't thought about pumping that beauty." He shook off Brian's scowling objection. "All you have to do is snap your fingers, big boy, and Jessica's on her back with her legs in the air reaching her arms out for her own wet dream personified. You two were meant to cause earthquakes! Don't tell me you don't want to fuck the hell out of her. God damn, what I would give to be in your place."

Brian hated Earnie's loud and crude assumption of his feelings. He glanced around to see if anyone was listening. He hated it, but the bastard had admirable insight.

"You're right."

"Don't give me that sh... What?"

"Oh hell, you're right, Earnie. But, geez! Who in their right mind wouldn't desire a night in that heaven?"

Earnie filled Brian's glass again. "Brian, are you all right? Can this really be my pristine brother?"

"I'm just saying that I've thought about her and me together. I wouldn't ever think of pursuing such a thought."

"Brian, don't piss me off."

Charlie came up the steps to the deck and bumped his head on the opening as he looked behind at Jessica. He came over to where Brian and Earnie were relaxing against the solid railing.

"Is that your friend?" he asked while rubbing his head.

"That's his secret lover," said Earnie.

"Oh, bullshit."

"Looks like you hit the jackpot, buddy. Pour me some of that." He held his glass out and Earnie poured. "She's driving the crew nuts below." He rubbed his hand on his head again.

"Fortunately you still have your sanity." Brian grinned when Charlie pulled his hand away.

"Let's take her out!" Donnie Bonito shouted, as best he could with his gentle and submissive voice. "Nigel, throw off the lines."

"We're going out on the ocean?" Earnie asked. "With them?"

Brian's giggle was hidden from the others by the purr of the diesel engine kicking in. Nigel stumbled aboard the moving craft with the last line. The champagne was making Brian lightheaded, and he watched with amusement Donnie directing his boyfriend Nigel around the deck with delicate hand waves and orders. Karen said they'd been living together for four years. It was probably the longest relationship that Donnie had ever managed. And Karen said they always seemed to get along fine, that they were actually a beautiful couple.

"What are you grinning about?" asked Charlie.

The girls coming topsides saved Brian from his thoughts. They watched, entranced, the beautiful parade: Marilee in her one piece rainbow on white Speedo; Natalie in green and Karen in light blue bikinis; Jessica in her orange patches. The men drooled shamelessly.

"You're going to step on your tongues," said Natalie before giving Charlie a kiss.

Marilee snuggled up to Earnie, and Karen leaned up against the superstructure.

"You throw a great party," Jessica shouted to Donnie who smiled and waved. "Does the captain mind a little nudity?"

Donnie looked at the others, and when Earnie shrugged and gave the thumbs up, Donnie shouted back at her, "So, go for it, darling."

As the others watched with open-mouthed amazement, she reached behind and untied the straps of her top. She gave Brian a quick smile and pulled it off.

"I'm getting some sun."

She walked carefully to the less crowded bow and sat, leaning back with her hands behind her head, on one of the secured deck chairs that Donnie had fortuitously added to his boat.

Karen and Natalie looked at each other and then laughed.

"Well, what the hell?" said Karen. Brian's amazement grew when they, too, reached back and released their tops. The two moved forward to lounge beside Jessica.

"It's got to be the champagne," said Brian.

"Who cares what it is," said Earnie. Marilee jabbed him in the side making him laugh and hug her tighter. "There's not even enough sun for a tan. That's pure exhibitionism."

"Bravo, that," said Brian.

They were far out of the harbor when Donnie and Nigel set the sails. That wonderful feeling was gripping Brian now. The motor was cut and the light wind they had found pushed at their ballooning spinnaker. He made his way up to sit between Karen's legs, with his back against her chair, and listened to the slap of water on the hull.

The meditative state put his mind at ease and made thinking clearer and easier. Thoughts of the post office surfaced, and a brighter picture was shaped out here than the one he conjured up under the cloud of disillusionment that engulfed him in that dark building. Out here, where he rolled along on the gentle swells under the open sky, that was another world, one that he could tuck away or observe from a safe and contented distance with compassionate clarity.

Chapter 7

On the edge of Encinitas the red-brick Santa Margarita Hospital sits sprawled in relative obscurity beneath the covering of a small forest of dozens of giant Eucalyptus trees. They shadow the sparse, root-permeated grounds, dark behind an old block fence laced over in heavy, gripping ivy vines. The massive and ancient building can barely be seen from the quiet, distant street passing by out front. There are typically few visitors, since the patients who live here ordinarily never leave.

When Tom stepped into the familiar, sanitized, Spartan room he saw that she was curled up in a ball in the middle of a wad of white sheets and blankets. He frowned at the nurse who followed him in.

"How long has she been like this?" he said in a low voice.

"She had another bad dream last night. She hasn't eaten or moved from the bed all day. She..." The nurse sighed.

"What?"

"Well...she...she had a visitor, too."

When Tom scowled at her, she took an instinctive step backwards.

"He's been here before. His mom is here in A-wing."

"Who?"

Tom continued to stare hard at her, and she fumbled at a clipboard in her hands while turning pages and glancing up at him.

"Leonard Nicks. His mom is Fiona Nicks. She's in A-wing. Oh, I guess I said that. I..." She stopped when she saw the look on his face.

"Did you guys dope her up again?"

"She was out of control, Tom," the nurse said defensively. "You know how she can get. She can't always separate fantasy from reality."

After an uneasy moment, Tom gave a brisk nod. "Leave us alone. Please," he added as he heard Sue stir. The nurse hesitated for a moment then stepped back, quietly pulling the door shut behind her.

Tom moved over to the bed and stood there. After a few moments, he sat on the edge of the bed. She rolled over to look at him through misty, faraway eyes. She focused more intently, then suddenly sat up and hugged him.

"It's OK," he said beginning to gently rock her. "It's good to see you, too, Sweet Sue."

"He was here, again!"

"I know."

"He told me that you are having a tough time at work. He said he worries about your state of mind."

"He what?"

"Don't you do anything like I did!" she said looking up at him.

Tom hesitated. He didn't want her to see his anger, but he was almost too furious to speak.

"Promise me!"

"You never have to worry about that. Ever. He's making it up, Sue. He's a bad one." He pulled her close again. "Really bad," he mumbled.

"I need to see people!"

"OK. I'm sorry. It's OK."

"You said he's a bad one."

"I understand; it's OK." He sighed, searching for words that would not hurt or confuse her. "Just be careful. When he tells you something like that, about me, or something that might hurt you or make you feel terrible, just wait for me."

"He would never hurt me."

Tom glared into a blinding void as he held her head against his chest, and he had to try again to calm himself down. He took a deep breath and said, "I'm the one who would never hurt you, Sue, honey. Come on, tell me; who's your number one?"

She pushed away and looked fearfully at him, clutching at his arms as if he might slip away. "You are! You have always been here for me when no one else cared. But I need to see other people, too!"

"I know. But be careful with that one. Can you do that for me? Whatever you hear, from anyone, always wait for me to tell you the truth. OK?"

She dug her head back into his massive chest and pulled him tight before nodding her head.

"Good. Now I can relax, too."

But he couldn't. There could be no good reason for the Weasel to be suddenly visiting Sue, and it worried him deeply. Something was going on, and it was wrong. But he didn't want her to worry, anymore, in her fragile condition. More than anything he wanted to take her as far away from her worries as he could take her. She had already overused her lifetime human ration of pain, and anything he could do to prevent any more anxiety in her life was worth any personal sacrifice he could ever make, even if it meant giving some temporary grace to one of the pricks who was trying to fire him.

"Hey, we just finished a football game with Carlsbad."

"Really? Who won?"

"We did."

"Was Brian there?" She looked up with anticipation and excitement. It made him feel good. One thing she enjoyed more than anything was listening to Tom's stories about the funny and interesting things that happened at work. It gave her a connection to a world she had become disconnected from. She knew the guys at work as well as Tom did just from the stories.

"Yes he was. And, oh my God! We have a new guy at work, now. His name is Earnie Franks."

"How about Jessica?"

"Yes!" Tom laughed. "That woman is crazy! She caught an amazing touchdown pass."

"Oh, my gosh I love her! She's so tough." Sue grinned at him. "She'll even stand up to you."

She yawned and snuggled into his arms.

"Tell me about the game."

"We usually lose to those guys..."

He rubbed a hand through her hair. She didn't deserve to be here. As far as he was concerned she had been tormented and crushed by that managerial cadre at Bay City, particularly Whipcracker. When she started working there she was a married, wide-eyed rookie; she and her husband were finally out on their own, having overcome financial and personal disasters, including the tragic loss of their baby to SIDS just six months before she started. Sure, they were struggling to keep the new house they had bought, but she was willing to put up with almost anything to keep this new-found financial independence and distraction from her recent heartbreak going. She needed to stay busy. When her husband lost his job almost as soon as she started hers, the burden of keeping up the new life and financing the new home fell to her. As much as he tried, he was unsuccessful in finding more work, and he was becoming more and more agitated, and times were hard on her.

So when Whipcracker targeted her, flooding her with unwanted attentions, she tried to delicately divert them so as not to jeopardize her new job. When he finally realized that she would never relent and he could never have her, he recruited his buddies the Weasel, Darrell Diamond and Phyllis Dunn to turn her already stressful life into a living hell. They turned harassing her into a sick game.

"The bastards started out cheating!" Tom said, more forcefully than he intended.

"Tom?" said Sue, looking up at him.

"Sorry. I got carried away. It was just for one play," he said. "It was actually kind of funny."

"How was it funny?" she asked, stressing 'funny' and making a face at him.

Tom smiled and rubbed a thumb gently along the length of one of her wrist scars. This was her time, now. There was time for worry later.

"They sewed their flags onto their belts, and Jimmy got pulled right along with the ball carrier after he grabbed on..."

She shook her head and smiled, snuggling up again. "Sewed them on? Oh, my. Poor Jimmy..."

No, Tom thought. *Poor fucking Weasel.*

Chapter 8

"The mutilated body of student and model, Amy Ventura, missing for two days, was discovered last night in a dumpster behind an Arizona State cafeteria, bringing to thirteen the number of women believed to have been murdered by Sterling Loudan, otherwise known as the Playboy Murderer."

It was Sunday morning, ten o'clock. Brian and Earnie watched Karen's Friday broadcast on Earnie's VCR. Karen was on assignment to god knows where, and Brian had come over to rehash the football game and the party. He was met instead by a resolute Earnie who insisted on showing Brian the tape.

"I was just talking to Sandrella McGunther this morning before you got here," he had said. "Those cops reminded me that I hadn't called her in quite a while." His look darkened, and he said, "Bay City was Sterling Loudan's home and place of business for a year and a half. L.A. was his playground, and Sandrella's business was one of his entertainment spots. How many people know that?"

Karen's broadcast continued with a push of the button:

"From witnesses' reports, Sterling Loudan had used the gymnasium the day before Amy Ventura's disappearance. As he has done in almost every other case, he discovered Ventura's campus address through conversations he struck up with students in the campus weight room. Ventura had posed as the centerfold of the February issue of Ballbuster Magazine. Evidence found at the scene and witness reports have implicated Loudan, who continues to evade nationwide law enforcement efforts to capture him.

"An unidentified source, close to his family in Pensacola, has shed some unusual light on the brutal murders. Loudan's wife, Amy, a onetime center folder herself, who still remains in police custody, starred in pornographic videos that were privately released just prior to Loudan's cross-country rampage. The source stated that Loudan had tried unsuccessfully to stop the release, and two as yet unsolved murders, that of Tom Wilson and Sasha Anderson, distributors of their own films, were tied to the release of the Amy Loudan videos. The FBI refused to comment on the story or the murders, which, if attributed to Loudan, would bring to fifteen the total number of known deaths related to the Playboy Murderer's still unchecked spree of horror."

"Everybody's always taping my wife."

Earnie stopped the video. Brian watched him walk over to the wall-sized map of the United States. He ran a finger from Pensacola, Florida, passing over the location of all the murder sights across country to Tempe, Arizona. His finger then continued slowly on to southern California. He turned and looked at Brian.

"See. He's on his way here."

"How long have you been doing this?"

"Ever since that night in the Leucadian." He began filing some of the clippings from the day's papers with those he'd already been saving or copied from the library. He flipped open a file and showed Brian a picture.

"Here; let me introduce you to the prick."

"This thing's gotten to you, hasn't it?"

Earnie shut the folder and tossed it down. "There's nothing I revere more in this world than a woman. Especially a beautiful woman." Brian followed him through the living room and out onto the veranda overlooking the ocean. "I just wish I could get my hands on the bastard."

"He's a pretty big bastard."

"Yeah." Earnie laughed the word as if to say, "So what?"

They made themselves comfortable on the wicker chairs next to the Jacuzzi that came with Earnie's rental and watched a woman, preparing to catch the early Sunday morning rays, spread a blanket on the sand far below.

"This must have come in my mail yesterday while we were playing football." Brian handed him the newsletter.

"What is it?" Earnie asked.

"It's about us."

He looked through it for a minute, and his glum disposition slowly changed. He laughed aloud, finally, and waved the newsletter at Brian.

"You son-of-a-bitch! You wrote this, didn't you?"

"I, uh, I cannot say."

"I'll bet I have one in my mailbox, too." He winked at Brian. "I should have checked this morning after taking Marilee home, but my mind was elsewhere.

"Injun Joe's?" He laughed again, looking at it. "What you have here is enough to shake up management big-time. Oh," he said pointing to the cartoon strip. "Weasel's going to love this." In the strip, Weasel had on an EEO button with a circle surrounding and a red bar running diagonally through the letters. He was sneaking a look at Jimmy Winfield tying a shoelace by a throwing case. A counter in the top right corner showed $0.00. The next frame showed Weasel whispering to Whipcracker and pointing to Jimmy's case, and the counter read $1,100.62. The third frame showed Weasel busy typing a letter of warning. He had a sign on his desk that said 'GOD,' and the counter read $3,712.18.

The final frame had a grinning Jimmy holding out a paper that said "Rather large bill for messin' with Jimmy the Untouchable," As his black rimmed glasses peeked over his shoulder, the Weasel was walking away with a scowl, stopped in the middle of his identifiable hitch. Jimmy was wearing a pin that said "I (with a picture of a heart) EEO," and he was pointing to the counter which now read $6,482.00.

"There's some clever stuff here. I like Whynaught's state of the post office message, "If you have a problem, come to me. But remember, if you can actually find me leave your problem at the door." Do you think you'll get away with this?"

"I can't say that I had anything to do with..."

"Ah, that's right. I forgot. That's your story and you're sticking to it. Believe me," Earnie grinned, "I wouldn't want you to say anything incriminating. I just can't wait to see the look on

Whipcracker and Weasel's faces Monday morning." He looked at the Injun Joe's newsletter again. "This doesn't sound like it was made up." He was pointing to the tape transcripts.

"Those are word for word. Or so I've heard."

"Yeah, right. Damn, they really want Tom Short out, don't they?"

"That's obvious just from work. But think of what those transcripts mean, legally speaking. Somebody's going to catch some hell."

"Yeah, but who?" Earnie grinned and threw his arms out. He read some more then stopped. "Oh, shit. They brought his girlfriend into it, too? How fucking sick are they?"

"She's not really his girlfriend; but, yeah, I'd say pretty sick."

Earnie looked some more, shaking his head. He finally threw the newsletter down and said, "It's too much to think about right now. Let's go grab a beer and talk about our next boat party."

*****

On Monday Whipcracker's face carried the fire-red glow of an early morning desert sun. Leonard "the Weasel" Nicks' lips had disappeared because, as Jimmy had said, his face was screwed up as tight as a duck's ass. He kept glancing at Jimmy who winked back several times. Phyllis Dunn clutched at her hands, and her blue and white face looked as if it had been cut out of ice. It was a ten-thirty Monday morning stand-up, and postmaster Whynaught, in a rare appearance, scratched his head and walked back and forth between the managers and clerks looking as confused as ever while looking through the copy of Injun Joe's that Phyllis had shoved into his hands. He looked up at her and she nodded her head sternly as if to say, "Get on with it, Henry!"

"OK, who wrote this?" That caused some immediate chuckling. Whynaught shrugged and grinned before nervously looking back at Phyllis.

"Henry!"

"Right!"

He quickly drew himself up, and after clearing his throat he addressed the group again as he continued to skim the newsletter.

"Uh; a lot of this is possibly illegal. There are libelous accusations, illegally acquired and fabricated conversations and... Hey! This isn't true!" He looked up like a sad-eyed puppy while tapping the newsletter, pleading with the clerks. "Come on you guys; you know you can come to me for help. Anytime."

"Yeah, if we can find you," Jessica said softly to Brian.

The laughter subsided when Phyllis stepped forward and snatched the newsletter away from the postmaster.

"What Henry is trying to say is people are going to pay for this. You can and will be fired for printing this trash. It's a bad—no; *disgusting* reflection of the postal service, all this criticism of management," she said shaking the newsletter, "and that makes it a violation of the Postal Service Code of Ethics." She jabbed it back at Whynaught. "Henry!"

"Yes, uh, thank you, Phyllis." He turned away quickly when she jerked her head back toward the clerks. "Oh!" He cleared his throat while waving the newsletter and said, "And now I'd like to ask whoever is responsible for this, this drivel, to step forward so they can, you know, face the music and all. All right? Who did it? One of you?" He looked intently at the quizzical faces and finally turned, satisfied, to address Phyllis. "Apparently not one of our crew."

"Of course it is!" she said ferociously over the mounting giggles. She turned and stormed back into her office.

"Well, uh, thank you for your time, people. I guess that's it. Unless..."

"Get your sorry asses back to work! But remember, damn it, someone is going to pay for that pack of lies!" Whipcracker had blown, and a meek Whynaught backed into the security of the hallway leading to his office.

"I don't even know what they're talking about," said Tom. He had started back out onto the dock.

"Me neither, man." Jimmy started laughing at Tom's comical look of innocence. "Two hours of mandatory overtime!" he blubbered before Whipcracker could get the words out of his own mouth.

"Someone's in trouble," said Brian. "But of course, you guys never said those things, right?"

Whipcracker was having a hard time focusing on anyone in particular. He stuck a finger in Brian's face and said, "I'd keep my nose clean, if I were you, buster!"

"Talk about the pot calling the kettle black," Anita de la Cruz said to Marilee while settling into her distribution stool.

"I heard that!"

"At least your ears are clean," said Brian. He dutifully headed toward the register cage.

Whipcracker stormed into Phyllis's office to the sound of laughter. Weasel glared at Jimmy and started back toward his carriers. Jimmy began singing some words he'd made up about "One Big Bill," causing Weasel to hitch up his step. Weasel suddenly stopped and came back to Brian.

"You're behind all of this, aren't you?"

"I'm afraid I don't know any more about what you're talking about than you ever do, Weasel."

"Don't call me Weasel!"

Brian looked puzzled for a moment and then said, "But that's your name, isn't it?"

Lenny, the ex-Weasel, walked away, unable to absorb any more of the abusive laughter.

For the rest of the morning, the supervisors laid low, staying out of sight of the razzing clerks as much as possible. But around noon Whipcracker stepped out onto the dock, and in a few minutes the sounds of Tom's angry roaring bit through the air. Whipcracker came in with a smug look on his face, followed by Phyllis Dunn, who had just returned from lunch. The satisfaction on their faces was enough to dampen the spirits of the clerks who watched them disappear into Phyllis's office.

"Shit," said Jimmy. "That don't look good."

Just when things were looking up, thought Brian.

"Here's the most recent up-to-date tally on Tom," said Ramon. "Three letters of warning, one removed, two on file; one administrative leave of nearly five days, dismissed as an overreaction by management; and one notice of suspension of two weeks, reduced to one—time not yet served. That's not counting discipline over two years old."

"What's next?" asked Brian.

"Two weeks' suspension, no reduction, and then possible removal, for the good of the service. Anything of a violent nature would be grounds for immediate removal pending the outcome of the grievance process."

"OK, let's get this straight," said Jessica. "Tom, even though he is a pervert, throws as much mail as anyone—when he gets a chance to since Whipcracker always has him on the dock dumping mail, which he does better than anyone—; he never misses work because of illness; he always does what he is told to do. What gives, Brian?"

"They're after him..."

"And the union can't do a damn thing about it," said Anita.

"'Fraid that's true," Jimmy piped in. "They didn't help me none. Too bad Tom ain't black. I'd turn him on to EEO."

"Well, he's not getting a fair shake as it is." Jessica turned on her stool to face Jimmy at his flat case. "He's obviously being discriminated against."

"But not due to race, age, sex, religion or any other helpful et ceteras."

"Then that's bullshit," said Jessica. She was angry and ferociously snapped letters into their pigeon holes. "He's not being protected because he's being discriminated against for something not on a list?"

"It isn't fair," said Brian. "There is only one way for Tom to beat management, and that is to wait them out through the grievance process. Unfortunately, they keep piling the garbage on, and Tom is not a very patient man."

"Even that's bullshit, Brian, if the union can't help him."

It was with a downbeat mood that the clerks began punching off the clock at one o'clock. Brian sat in the swing room taking his first break of the day and wished he were going home, too. He listened to Tom explaining rather loudly about how he had supposedly threatened Whipcracker again, and how "that ice-bitch," Phyllis Dunn, had snuck up and became a witness to threats that had never taken place. He ignored Bill Rose's comments concerning grieving the notice of suspension that was forthcoming.

"The union hasn't been any more help than that idiot postmaster we've got. Goddamn it, today I'm buying that gun!" Tom literally punched the clock and left.

Jessica stopped by the swing room on her way out the door for the day. She smiled at Brian and came over and sat beside him. She opened her mouth to speak then closed it and sighed. Finally she spoke.

"You know, Brian, it's really hard to make a pass under these conditions. Something screwy happens every day in here."

Brian remembered what she had looked like in—and out—of that orange bikini on Donnie Bonito's sailboat Saturday. It had been the exclamation point on what Earnie had been urging him to do with her. His body heated up as she continued.

"Brian, I want to go out with you. Maybe it could work out, maybe not. I don't want to step on Karen's toes, or hurt you—especially hurt you. But damn it, let's find out sometime." They looked at each other in silence for a moment. She smiled and said, "Sorry, I'm not good at saying this. It's the first time that I ever asked a guy out. Usually it's the other way around. And I'm the one saying no.

"Oh hell, Brian. It doesn't have to be anything serious." She stood up suddenly. "It's just that I'm attracted to you, and I think you're attracted to me." She started to leave.

"You know what? There's so much going on lately," said Brian, and that stopped her at the door. "It's so overwhelming and confusing. I mean like Tom wanting to buy a gun, for crying out loud. That's a little scary. By the way; do you know how crazy Earnie is over the Playboy Murderer? He's got a map that covers an entire wall! And Karen's so busy with her network news that she's seldom home anymore. I don't think I've seen her for more than five minutes at a time in a week. And our pitiful life in here just goes on. So many things going on."

"You ever want to talk," said Jessica, "Or anything—let me know." She smiled when Brian nodded his head. "You don't have to play so hard to get."

Brian watched her leave. Earnie walked in with his lunch pail and sat across from him. He had watched her go down the hall on the way out the door.

"I swear, she's one fine-looking woman. I can't understand why she wants you and not me."

"Let's talk about something else, huh?"

"Sure, Brian. What's on your mind? That you want to talk about, I mean?" He looked out the door. "Like, how was the stand-up?"

"Whynaught couldn't handle it, so Phyllis took over. They were all pissed off about Injun Joe's."

"But they don't really know who wrote it?" Earnie chomped on a peanut butter and jelly sandwich.

"No, but outside of pissing them off, I don't know what good it's going to do. I thought we had something good with it. But Whipcracker went after Tom about an hour ago out on the dock. And as luck would have it, Phyllis was just around the corner. I think they're going to suspend him."

"Luck had nothing to do with it," said Earnie with a mouth full of sandwich. "I'll bet Tom was pissed."

"He said again, for about the millionth time, that he's going to buy a gun."

"You can do that in America."

"As much as he talks about it, I'm afraid he's serious this time. He showed me pictures of some foreign automatic machine gun he's in love with."

"Then I hope he's not pissed at me."

"Me either." Brian got up to go back to work. "I hope that's all he's doing—just making threats."

"And I hope I'm not around when he blows."

Brian walked back to the register cage. As he began logging registers he thought, it's happened before. And the fool in that case was shooting everyone. I hope that if Tom goes nuts, he's at least selective about his targets. Brian flashed a grim smile at that macabre thought. He didn't have much compassion for some of the people he worked for.

He thought about what Jessica had said to him, and as he always did when he thought about her, he began to feel a tug of war between exhilaration and guilt. He did want her. And she wanted him. So why not? Maybe he would get too involved, or get her too involved. Whoever knew about how these things would turn out? Maybe Karen would find out. Then how badly would she be hurt? Lots of maybes. The biggest one was maybe he couldn't handle the guilt. Because one thing he was certain of—it was wrong, and he shouldn't even be thinking about it.

But he did, and the more he thought about it, the more he wanted it to happen. You'll never know unless you try, the bad little voice in his head was saying, although, Brian suspected, it was getting the source of its feelings from his loins. Besides, what he had let slip out to Jessica was true. Karen was so busy building her reputation and career that lately she'd been neglecting his needs. In the past month, they'd made love only about four or five times and that was becoming the norm. Hell, he thought, before she became the noon anchor at KMAA, doing that in a good weekend had not been out of the question. Now she was shooting for co-anchor on the evening news, and because of her hard work, she would probably get it. But the price of her success was causing a lot of personal emptiness and frustration in his life.

I'm thinking too much. I shouldn't worry about the guilt. Karen already has a lover—her work. At least it's something she does love. He thought about his own work and shook his head. Physically fine—mentally depressing. Thanks to the Whip, Weasel, Dunn and Diamond. I hope Tom gets them, he thought before immediately deciding he didn't want anyone shot, not even those assholes. It was funny that Diamond had stayed so clear of the stand-up. "Check the door." He was too much of a chicken-shit to be visibly involved with that group.

While Brian organized his registers early for the evening dispatch, he decided, finally, that yes, he was going to take Jessica up on her generous offer.

Chapter 9

The next day it was a big surprise to everyone to find that Tom hadn't been suspended. The day after the Injun Joe's stand-up and Tom's most recent run-in with Whipcracker, Bill Rose, as union president, and Tom Short held a meeting with Postmaster Whynaught, assistant Postmaster Phyllis Dunn and Supervisor Whipcracker to discuss the allegations against Tom. The meeting lasted just over two hours. Rose took a calculated risk, pointing out the fact that this suspension, coming on the heels of the surreptitious publication of Injun Joe's, could cause some real publicity and stunk of a set-up anyway.

Whynaught, mindful of the possible disruption of his quiet and secluded little world, bought into the argument, agreeing with Rose's arguments over the objections of Dunn and Whipcracker. He was, from the beginning, at his agreeable best, agreeing with everyone's points of view, but he finally was worn down by Rose's persistent emphasis on the publicity the union would create if this wasn't resolved in Tom's favor. And right now. Rose wouldn't leave any room for Whynaught's patented wriggling and sidestepping of the issue and demanded his resolution in writing.

At the end of the meeting, everyone looked worn out except Tom, who swaggered out with a huge grin saying, "Free—I'm free at last!"

The clerks were astounded when they found out the result. Brian went up to the front window to pick up registers and the signed collection slips and to tell Earnie. There were no other customers in line and Earnie was talking with a tall, golden-haired, green-eyed woman who's substantially conspicuous breasts seemed to be considering escape from the V-necked white sweater that contained them. Acting busy, from nearby, he listened in.

"I guess I've never found the right woman."

"Well then, you just might not be gay," she said. "You said you're not sure."

"But how will I ever know?" he asked sadly. "I've never touched a man—not yet. But I just don't know. The few women I've been with seemed to use me as an object to satisfy their own cravings, leaving me spent but empty inside. How will I ever know the truth?"

Brian shook his head and grinned.

"OK," she said firmly, "I want you to meet me Friday at this address." She wrote it down on Earnie's scratch pad. "We'll just see how much of what persuasion you really are. And if what I have planned doesn't straighten out your thinking, then we'll know for sure. All right?"

"Oh, thank you," said Earnie. "I've got to know. I'll be there. Thank you."

"Don't thank me now," she said. "Just don't decide not to show up on Friday." She started to leave then turned back toward him. "You've got to give women one more chance."

"I will," he said delicately, and she smiled and strolled out.

"Whoa!" he said to Brian. "Is Samantha gorgeous or what?"

Brian was impressed by the woman, and he watched her until she turned out of sight through the lobby doors. He looked at Earnie and shook his head.

"How the hell do you find beautiful women that'll buy your bullshit?"

"It's like hypnotism—you can't do anything that's morally or ethically against your personal or subconscious feelings. She wanted me all along but needed a reason to follow through."

"You're going to have to report back on this one."

"What happened in the meeting?" Being at the front counter caused Earnie to miss the stand-ups and much of what went on in the back.

"Tom got off."

"No suspension?"

"No suspension, no letter of warning, nothing."

"How did he manage that?"

"Bill Rose convinced Whynaught that there would be a lot of adverse publicity if Tom was suspended especially so close to the publication of Injun Joe's. He told them that it stunk of a set-up, anyway."

"It was the publicity bit that got to that mole, Whynaught, wasn't it?"

"I think so."

"Could there have actually been any publicity over it?"

"I don't know; but Whynaught was convinced, and that's all that mattered."

A man stepped up to the counter. Brian began scooping up signed notices and the letters out of Earnie's register drawer.

"I'd like a money order for one hundred dollars."

Earnie cut him the money order and the man paid for it.

"Now I'd like to register this in a letter to Japan."

"Oh, they won't cash a domestic money order in Japan, sir."

"What?" The man looked at Earnie with irritation. "Then I guess this is no good." He ripped the money order into pieces with amazing speed while Brian and Earnie watched in astonishment.

"Sir," said Earnie finally. "Sir. The domestic money order could have been cashed or traded in for an international money order."

The man held the last remaining pieces in his hands and watched a few pieces sift through his fingers and float to the floor.

"What?"

"That money order was still good as cash."

"Why didn't you tell me?"

Earnie laughed out loud at the man's pitiful expression. He reached for the scotch tape. "Here, put it back together the best you can and I'll figure something out." The man took the tape and began picking up the pieces. When he had them all, he went across to one of the customer counters.

"He's got some work in front of him," Earnie said with a grin.

"You get them all, don't you?" said Brian. "Beautiful women with some extra entertainment tossed in. I should have been a window clerk."

"You've got your own entertainment in the back," said Earnie. "Although it often borders on the darkness of an Ingmar Bergman movie."

"Tell me about it."

Earnie laughed then asked, "Hey, do you think you can get free this weekend?"

"Lately I've been free every weekend," Brian said wistfully. "Karen just comes home in time to go to sleep."

"Then come with me to my old stomping grounds up in L.A. I've got to trade my old clunker in to an honest old buddy who sells used cars."

"Sounds good to me. I'm tired of giving you a ride home every few days while your car's in the shop."

"How do you think I feel, throwing my life into your hands on the back of a two-wheeler?"

"Safe as a kitten in a basket?"

"More like Evil Knievel's shadow."

When Brian went to the back, Tom was telling Ramon about his new semiautomatic AK-47 assault rifle he had just picked up and the kit he had sent for to convert it into an automatic. They were near the time clock preparing to punch off and go home.

"I bought it yesterday. I've been talking to this guy and decided it was time."

"You actually got it?"

"Yeah, and I got two hundred rounds of ammunition with it."

"So, you taking it duck hunting, or what?" asked Ramon.

"Supervisor hunting," he said. "Come on out to my truck and take a look." He punched off the clock just as Whipcracker stepped out of the office hallway where he'd been standing.

"You have a gun on postal property?"

Tom stood staring owl-like at Whipcracker through his black framed glasses.

"I heard you say you had an assault rifle in your truck. Do you?" Tom still stared. "Phyllis!"

She came out of her office and over to the time clock.

"This man has a weapon—a rifle—in his truck. And he has threatened to shoot a supervisor with it."

The clerks were stunned into silence.

"Call the postal inspectors," said Phyllis. "And you stay right there, Tom. The rest of you, if you have punched off, go home."

The other clerks left, whispering and glancing back. In a few seconds Bill Rose came in from the dock where he had been apprised of the situation by the departing clerks. Whipcracker bounced out of the office. Brian worked slowly on some C.O.D. second notices from a corner of the cage where he could listen in.

"Why are you detaining this man?"

"Because he has made threats to seriously endanger postal employees with a weapon he has in his truck," said Phyllis. "Are they on their way?"

"They'll be here in twenty or thirty minutes," said Whipcracker cheerfully.

For the next half hour, Rose argued the legality of detaining Tom and searching his property for an 'alleged' weapon. He silenced Tom once when he began to speak, and Tom remained quiet, although obviously shaken up, until the two inspectors arrived. Phyllis and Whipcracker talked to the tall inspector off to the side while the other exchanged dirty looks with Bill and Tom.

"OK," said the tall inspector. "Let's have a look in that truck."

"Huh uh," said Bill. "Not without a search warrant."

"That truck is on government property and subject to search at any time," said the tall inspector. "We don't need a search warrant."

"I'm afraid you have your wires crossed. You can't just waltz out and inspect someone's car anytime you want to. Can you inspect a customer's car without a warrant just because he's parked on postal property?"

The inspectors huddled with Phyllis and Whipcracker, and the short one broke off into the office. He came back in a moment and nodded his head.

"OK," said the other. "The warrant is being processed. Happy now?"

"No. I don't think you can make Tom wait here. Tom, don't say a word; I'll be right back."

Bill went into the swing room where the pay phone hung on the wall. Tom stared down the two inspectors until Bill returned.

"Tom, go home," he said.

"He can't go," said Phyllis.

"He is being illegally detained according to the lawyer I just called."

"Bullshit!" said Whipcracker.

"Tom, are you off the clock?"

"Yes, I am."

"Then get out of here, for Christ sake, unless you love this place so much you can't find it in your heart to leave. Get going."

While the inspectors objected, Tom grinned. He turned at the door and gave a friendly wave.

Brian watched the inspectors and supervisors leave frustration in their wake as they slunk into the office.

Tom sure knew how to get himself into bad situations, Brian thought. He was very happy Tom had gotten off, though. He went back to the front of the cage to begin checking in one of the early arriving carriers.

*****

At about seven-thirty, Brian leaned over his motorcycle to get the mail out of his mailbox. When he turned it around to go back up his driveway the motor stalled, and because of the angle he was on, the bike went down. He looked around and saw that no one was watching him. With some effort and embarrassment, he righted the bike and rode it up the driveway.

Inside the apartment he turned on the telephone message machine.

"I'm sorry, Brian. I've got to work late again because I have another story on the late news. I love you, honey, and I miss you. There's a TV dinner in the freezer. Again, I'm really sorry."

Brian picked up the phone and dialed.

"Hello?"

"Hi. It's Brian."

"Hi, Brian. What's up?"

"Do you, uh, mind if I come over? To talk?"

"No, of course not, dear."

"Give me about a half hour, OK?"

"Sure. I'll see you then."

The phone clicked, and Brian slowly set it down.

Forty minutes later, after a shower and shave, Brian pulled into Jessica's driveway. She owned a small tract home down a quiet cul-de-sac. She met him at the door in her bathrobe. A huge Great Dane shoved its nose past her to inspect the stranger.

"Get back, Bjorn. Hi, Brian."

"I hope I'm not disturbing you."

"Oh, stop it. And come on in." Bjorn sniffed at him when he stepped in, then went into another room after deciding the stranger was no danger to his master. "I was just reading when you called."

He stood in the hallway, and Jessica smiled at him.

"I know how you must feel, you poor boy." She took his hand and led him into the living room. The shades were drawn, and champagne jazz played on her stereo. She turned to face him and said, "Thank you for coming over." She gave him a kiss.

He didn't resist, and in a moment, as her robe fell open, his arms slid around her.

*****

The night air blew through Brian's hair, and the Suzuki vibrated and roared between his legs. He had showered at Jessica's, and he felt clean and relaxed. What had just happened was like a dream—like it hadn't really happened. What he couldn't understand was his lack of any feelings of guilt. Jessica had made the whole thing seem natural, even expected of him. His pleasure had been as great as hers. Once, while they had languished in the afterglow of a round of lovemaking, she had said, "Just don't forget—I'm here, anytime you want to...talk."

He rode up the driveway. Karen was still not home. She would probably be at least another hour if she was going to make the late news. She puts in long hard hours, he thought. I just hope that she enjoys what she's doing and gets what she's searching for.

Brian suddenly realized he was starving. He took the TV dinner from the freezer and tossed it into the microwave.

Chapter 10

The next morning Brian awoke disconcerted from an uneasy night's sleep. Despite his restlessness, he hadn't heard Karen come in the night before or get up in the morning. But she was milling about in the kitchen. He went in to investigate. She had poured him some cereal and orange juice. She smiled at him and popped some burned toast out of the toaster.

"You're making breakfast?"

"You deserve it," she said. "You're a good husband, putting up with me like you have over these past few months."

Brian sat down and stared at his cereal. Karen brought the toast over with some milk and gave him a kiss.

"I'm sorry for the way things have been," she said. "But opportunities are looking much better for me at work. It won't be long before I'm on a regular schedule again. I realize I haven't been fair to you, lately.

"Are you all right, honey?" she asked.

"Yes," said Brian, snapping his head up. "Just a little tired."

"Well, I've got some good news and some bad news. Donnie said you could borrow the sailboat this weekend, if you'd like." She paused, and not getting the expected response, went on. "The bad news is I've got a meeting Saturday and have to work."

Brian spooned some cereal up to his mouth and before shoving it in said, "That's great."

"That's great?" Karen sat down beside him. "There is something wrong, isn't there, honey?" She put a hand on his shoulder and gave a gentle squeeze. "I'm really sorry that I haven't been a good wife, lately. I mean it. I love you so much. Things will get better, I promise."

Brian leaned over, put his arms around her and gave her a kiss. He didn't want his disconcerting behavior to upset Karen—he loved her, too.

"Things at work have me screwed up," he said. "I'm just getting really sick of it all."

"Then the sail is what you need!" she said.

It slowly dawned on him the more he thought about it, that it was true. Karen, Jessica, Earnie and the Playboy Murderer, Tom Short and the asshole supervisors. Time for the sea breezes to blow the conflicts away and cleanse his mind. Maybe he could sort it all out after such a purification.

"Does Charlie know, yet?"

"No," said Karen, brightening up to Brian's interest. "Why don't you give him a call at work?"

Brian continued eating his breakfast. He determined that the dullness he felt was a panacea meant to cover the edges of guilt that had finally begun to creep up on him. Women! How the hell do they know how to do it? The timing must be of great importance in playing a tune on a man's emotions, and somehow they never missed a cue.

After breakfast, he went to the phone and dialed Charlie at his office and was connected through his extension.

"Hey, Charlie, would you like to go sailing this weekend?"

"Shit! I've got system transfers to do Saturday."

"What does that mean?"

"It means I can't make it. It's crucial work that has to be done at that time and that time only." There was a pause on Brian's end, and Charlie asked, "What's wrong, Mr. Christian?"

"Oh, nothing really. Just wanted to talk. It would have been just you and me. A little overnight sail."

"Arr! Two lonely pirates on the open sea, maybe a bottle of rum and a few maids to lee? Shit!" He thought for a moment and said, "We'll get together when you get back Sunday. Then we'll talk. Hey, maybe you can ask Earnie to go."

"Mmm," said Brian. "I might do that."

"Well, I've got to get back to saving the computer world. Thanks for asking, Brian. And I'll catch you on the next trip."

After Charlie hung up, Brian hopped into the shower and got ready for work. He dressed, and Karen told him he had a phone call. She had a puzzled look on her face.

"It's the Blade-Tribune," she said.

"What?" He took the phone and said hello.

"Hi! Brian McGraw? This is Pat Divers of the Blade. I've got a copy of a newsletter called Injun Joe's. Does that ring a bell?"

"Yeah, it came out at work a few days ago. How did you get my number?"

"A list of phone numbers was dropped in my mailbox at home with that newsletter, and yours was one of seven numbers that was underlined. You're the first one I've been able to get hold of."

"What's this all about?"

"That's what I want to know, Mr. McGraw. Do you know who published Injun Joe's? Or how much is truth or fiction?"

"Listen Pat—Pat Divers? I would like to comment on all of this, but I could get in lots of trouble for making any public statements about post office issues."

"I understand! I'll give you and anyone else who will talk to me guaranteed anonymity. As a matter-of-fact, I'll take your names to jail with me if it actually comes to that. I smell a story, especially from the "Private Meetings" transcript in your newsletter. You know, about Tom Short."

"I didn't say it was my newsletter," said Brian. But he was getting excited about the prospect of a real newspaper picking up the story and going public. "Let me talk to some people, and I'll get back to you."

"Smart move. Ask for Pat Divers. And call soon. Here's my number and extension. Do me a favor and don't talk to anyone else at the Blade in case we have to keep this on the down-low." He gave Brian his telephone number, and Brian hung up the phone. Karen studied him with a quizzical look.

"A Pat Divers, from the Blade, wants the story on Tom and Injun Joe's. Can that writer guarantee anonymity?"

"A lot of it depends on his own integrity and the impact of the story and what kind of damage is involved."

"What do you think?"

"I'll find out about him at work today and let you know. Some of our reporters and theirs cross paths on different stories. Even though TV reporters and newspapermen don't always get along with each other, there's a mutual respect for certain writers. And I think I remember him as one you can trust."

"Thanks, honey." Brian threw on his jacket and grabbed his helmet. "I'm late for roll call."

"I love you, Brian," said Karen. She gave him a long kiss. "I wish you could quit that damned job."

He held her tight and said, "Aw, it's not so bad. It would just be nice having fair and respectful people running the show."

"I don't like seeing you unhappy. And I wish I were more help," she added. "I don't ever want to lose you, Brian." She kissed him again. "I hope you realize how much I love you."

When Brian hopped on his bike and started for work, he was just going through the motions. The wind did little to sort out his thoughts, today. He pulled his knees in against the gas tank when the chilled air penetrated his clothes. It was getting cold again. The overcast sky hung low over the ocean, reflecting Brian's gloom, and he took no notice of the time. He was ten minutes late. Whipcracker had his time card.

"Late again, McGraw."

"Yeah, sorry," Brian said reaching for his card. The clock clicked past another minute, and Whipcracker handed it to him. "Now I'm even later." He punched on.

"I think we'll get a letter of warning out of this, eh, McGraw?" He had an evil grin on his face. Tom Short and Ramon Lopez watched out of the corner of their eyes from nearby flat cases. Marilee Willing and Anita de la Cruz were doing likewise from their letter cases. Jessica sat with a handful of letters openly staring.

"Whatever."

"Oh, whatever, huh? Don't forget, you're on the clock this time if you decide you want to get lippy again." Whipcracker crossed his arms and rocked back on his heels. Brian stepped past him toward the cage. "Whatever happened to the defiant one?"

"Just type the goddamn thing, and I'll sign it!"

Whipcracker threw his hands up in mock surprise. But before he could say anything, Jessica spoke.

"Leave him alone. Can't you see he doesn't want to argue with you?"

Whipcracker's face flared momentarily. He stepped toward her and said, "Why don't you just get back to work, Miss America?"

"Why don't you ever knock off your bullshit and let us?" Jessica seemed close to tears. "Every day we've got to put up with this bullshit."

"Well, you don't have much of a choice, do you, you little bitch?"

"What?" said Marilee, stunned.

"Fucking asshole," said Jimmy under his breath.

Whipcracker swung around to Tom. "What did you say?"

"Someone called you a fucking asshole," Tom said. "I was only thinking it."

"I said it," Jimmy said defiantly.

"I said it," said Anita de la Cruz. She put a hand on Jessica's shoulder to comfort her. "And you are."

"Fucking asshole," said Brian.

"Fucking asshole," said Ramon.

Whipcracker turned from one to another unable to respond before each comment was fired. His face was red as a stoplight. He focused on Jessica's sobbing. "Is everyone sticking up for the cute little crybaby? Aww—did we hurt our feelings now?"

He reached over and pushed Anita's hand off Jessica's shoulder roughly replacing it with his own hands, pulling Jessica backwards and nearly off her stool. "When we grow up, things can get rough in the real world, little baby," he growled.

"Fuck you, cocksucker!" she said throwing his hands off her shoulder after regaining her balance.

At the same time Brian roared, "Get your hands off of her," and started around the cage. Before he could get to them, Tom had already grabbed Whipcracker by the neck and thrown him violently to the floor.

Brian grabbed Tom and screamed, "You motherfucker!" at Whipcracker.

Whipcracker, with a frightened look, was crawling frantically backwards toward the office where Phyllis Dunn had run out. She helped him to his feet. They disappeared into her office.

Bill Rose came running in just when Weasel darted past the group to the office. Jimmy and Ramon explained to Bill what had happened while Bill paced back and forth keeping himself strategically positioned between a snorting, agitated Tom and the office hallway. Jessica was being comforted by Anita and Brian. She was visibly shaken up.

Brian hugged her tight when she stood up and said, "I'm sorry. I should have hit him myself."

"It's not your fault," he said. "What the hell is wrong with him?" He saw the faces of other clerks and carriers peeking down the aisle to see what the commotion was all about. A hollow feeling inside of him momentarily crowded out the anger and fear, and he found his own comfort with her in his arms.

"Maybe she should go home," suggested Anita.

"You're right," said Brian.

"No, I'm all right," Jessica said, toughening back up.

Earnie came around the corner and said, "Geez, what happened? Two boys in blue just came through the front door and straight into the office."

He didn't have to wait long for an answer. They were led out of the office by Phyllis Dunn and the Weasel with a subdued Whipcracker in tow.

"That's the one," said Phyllis, pointing at Tom.

The policemen slowly looked Tom up and down and then at each other. "We may need a back-up."

"He was only protecting her," said Bill Rose, nodding toward Jessica, "From the violent and unwarranted advances of that man right there, Supervisor Whipcracker."

"You'd expect that from the union president," said Phyllis.

"And he called her a bitch!" Marilee stammered.

"It's true!" said Ramon.

"It is not!" said Phyllis. "I saw what happened, myself."

The clerks objected that she'd only seen the tail-end of what had really happened, and Phyllis yelled, "Get back to work!" She said to the police, "I'm in charge in this office, and I've ordered that man removed from the premises."

"You've got to leave, sir."

"This is the first time he's been asked to leave," said Bill. "And he will be happy to comply." He pulled at Tom's arm.

"Are they arresting me?" he asked.

"Of course not, Tom. What for?" said Bill. "Our bosses are just overreacting, as usual."

"Overreacting! He attacked me!" Whipcracker yelled. "Aren't you going to arrest him?" Tom scowled, and Whipcracker leaped back behind Phyllis.

"We have no justifiable reason to arrest him."

"So, let's go home, Tom." Bill tugged at his arm again. "You've got to go."

Tom looked at Whipcracker, and at the policemen, and down at Bill. "All right."

Bill led him out of the building.

"I guess we weren't needed, ma'am."

"Thanks a lot, you damn fools," said Whipcracker, stepping from behind Phyllis. He addressed the clerks. "Now get your butts back to work! I said now!"

Phyllis led the confounded policemen back to her office. And Whipcracker stormed in behind them.

Brian rubbed Jessica's shoulders when she sat back down at her case. "Are you OK?"

He was glad to hear her say, "If he ever touches me again, I'll kick his balls in." He went back into the cage and saw Earnie's questioning look. Brian asked him what he thought.

"They'll fire Tom for that," said Earnie.

"They should fire Whipcracker. He instigated the whole thing by grabbing Jessica like he did in front of all of us."

"We should probably pin a medal on Tom. He was just protecting the woman he loves to hate." He stared at Brian with that same quizzical look. "You're not jealous, are you?"

Brian felt his face warming. He said, "Would you like to go sailing this weekend? We can get your new car some other time."

"And maybe talk about Jessica? Not to change the subject." Earnie grinned when Brian started to object. "OK—if we make it through the week—sounds good to me. Talk to you later. I've also got to tell you about my grope therapy coming up with Samantha on Friday night. What a fine looking therapist! I've got to get up front. Let me know if anything else happens back here." He turned and left.

Brian went perfunctorily back to work preparing uncollected C.O.D.'s to return to senders. He saw Bill Rose go into the offices. After a few minutes he came out and asked Jessica to follow him into the swing room. Twenty minutes later she came out and told Anita to go in.

"Brian?"

He moved over to where Jessica was leaning between the divider in her throwing case, and he talked to her through the wire wall of the register cage.

"What's going on?" he asked.

"Oh, Bill's just taking our statements about what happened. They're going to fire Tom, but Bill thinks the union can have him reinstated after all the facts are out."

"What a mess."

She lowered her voice to a whisper. "Thank you for our little talk last night. I wanted to tell you that this morning."

His doubts about their affair took a sudden backseat to her sweet and candid innocence. He smiled and said, "My pleasure."

"It was more than a talk," she said. "It was more like the Gettysburg address. Uh oh; I'm getting all warm inside, again."

For the moment, Brian could imagine more of the magic of last night. In a flash, she had successfully erased the turmoil inside of him, but the only thing he could clearly see now was why so many men and even entire civilizations had fallen to the beauty of a woman.

"Thank you, Jessica, for more than just that talk." He liked the way "talk" had become a euphemism for their lovemaking.

He looked around and realized that this wasn't the best place to discuss their night or their future.

"Let's talk some other time."

"Sure, Brian. And let's make it soon." She winked and sat up straight in her lean-to and began firing letters into their respective pigeonholes.

He stepped back to the C.O.D.'s without trying to explain that he meant "talk" in the literal sense. Besides, he thought, it was the figurative "talk" that he wanted to talk about, anyway.

*****

Bill soon called him into his makeshift office in the swing room where he had papers scattered all over the table. Brian wrote out his statement on what he saw of the earlier occurrence and signed his name to the bottom with the date. He asked what was happening to Tom.

"He's been placed in off-duty status and indefinitely suspended from the postal service. Pending the outcome of this grievance, he's in limbo."

"Which means?"

"You might say he's been fired. All we can do is try to get him reinstated."

"Is that likely?"

Bill looked at Brian and said, "Honestly, not with his record. I think the bastards have succeeded this time."

Brian picked up his statement. "Then what good is this bullshit?"

"Tom's past record of discipline is not good. The fact that he has spoken of a gun and of shooting a supervisor is not good. But the possibility exists that he'll get a fair arbitrator down the line who will question some of management's zeal and procedures in their approach to disciplining him. And a second grievance will be filed against Whipcracker by the union for abusing, physically and verbally, Jessica this morning. With that we might force his removal from the supervisory ranks."

"And he'd be on the workroom floor with us?"

"Yes, that's possible, unless he's transferred out. Which is very possible under the circumstances. But even then it's more than likely he'll just end up with some kind of a suspension."

"I'd love to get my hands on him," Brian growled. He realized that he sounded like Earnie talking about the Playboy Murderer. "If Tom hadn't gotten to him first, I would have hit him this morning."

Bill looked surprised. He said, "That's why they would probably transfer him out if he loses. You would have hit him?"

"Swear to God."

Bill began picking up his papers and shoving them into his briefcase.

Brian said, "A man from the Blade called me this morning before work. They were asking about Injun Joe's."

Bill looked at him. "What did you say?"

"That I would get back to him. He said he wanted to contact about six or seven of us. He said he would guarantee anonymity."

Bill shuffled his papers thoughtfully. A smile came to him slowly, and he said, "Let's let him know. Everything. Let's let everyone know about this place, this paradise in the sun. We'll get his guarantee in writing. Give me his number and I'll pass it around. Hah! I'll tell Tom to call him. He can even use Tom's name, now! If worse comes to worst, I'll tell you, Brian, the post office is not the only game in town. None of us are as locked in to this job as we may think."

Now Brian was staring at him with an odd expression. "Mr. Straight-line Conservative? Is that really you?"

"Hell, I'm sick of this bullshit, too, Brian. I've been president of the local for the past nine years simply because no one else wanted the job. I've learned how to communicate with Whynaught to the extent that I know what we can get away with at steps one and two, and what we can't. I'm tired of sending grievances out of this office to step three just to have them sent back 'resolved in favor of management.' Compared to others, we're only a small office with a small voting record for national officers and issues—they don't give a shit about us at that level. If our grievances don't get resolved in the office, they don't get resolved at all. The big boys are too busy waxing the big locals' behinds, and we're just smalltime. And, shit, I'm only the man in the middle, a guy everyone can vent their frustration on, from union member to management. I'm only the front man for a group of people who are pretty much on their own.

"Hell, yeah, let's talk to that guy from the Blade! I've already threatened our local management with publicity, and I'd like to have some satisfaction for a change if only that of having the public know that everything isn't so wonderful here in paradise."

Brian let him rant on, mostly surprised by his outburst. When Bill had finished, Brian stood up and said, "I appreciate all you've done for us, Bill. I know it's a thankless job, and you've worked hard at it." He patted Bill on the shoulder. "Karen's going to find out how reliable this Pat Divers is. If he's OK, I'll let you know."

"Great. Mean time I'll keep this paperwork floating. Send in Ramon for me. And thanks."

When Brian got home that evening, he switched on the message machine. Karen assured him that Pat Divers was reliable and honest according to the people she worked with who knew him. She told him that there was a frozen pizza in the freezer, and that she loved him.

He threw the pizza into the microwave, and while it was heating up he dialed the Blade and asked for Pat Divers. He picked up the extension immediately.

"Mr. McGraw! I've been getting great feedback from your co-workers. Thank you for letting them know I was interested in their problems at work. And, oh, what an assortment of problems! Whatever happened to a non-hostile work environment?"

Brian thought his co-workers might have jumped the gun in talking to Divers before getting the report on his reliability, but he said, "I'm glad to help, Pat. I don't know what you can do about it, but maybe publicity can help us sort out that mess. It's only getting worse."

"Yes, but I'm sure that the adverse publicity in this article will shake their socks loose. It'll be good reading, and it might even help you guys out." Pat sounded excited at the prospects of his story. "I'm going to do a two-parter, Friday and Sunday. Your local union president, Bill Rose, was very helpful."

Brian laughed and said, "That tells you how bad things are going right there."

For the next half hour they discussed the post office, past and present. While he chewed on a piece of pizza, Brian admitted he was part of the publication of Injun Joe's, and explained why he felt its conception had become necessary and how it now appeared to have been a useless gesture since Tom Short had likely been fired anyway. Pat told him he had been shocked to find out that the transcribed meeting had actually taken place.

"Your Mr. Ramon Lopez, who, by the way, contributed a lot of facts, has assured me I could have a copy of that tape. Three people, including you, have sworn to its authenticity."

"It's real, all right. We just can't use it."

"I'll talk to our lawyer on this information I've gathered to make sure I present it in a protected, legal manner. I thank you again, Brian. All I have left is to straighten it all out into permissible and interesting copy, and I think we'll have a winner."

"One question," Brian asked. "Who sent you a copy of Injun Joe's in the first place?"

"That's a funny thing," said Pat. "It was addressed to me at my home, and no one gives out my home address. It was folded like a letter, and where the return address should have been was a pair of artistically and beautifully drawn eyes. The accompanying sheet of phone numbers, with certain numbers underlined had a simple four word message—'better check this out.' It was too intriguing to pass up, and I'm glad I didn't."

They disconnected after goodbyes, and Brian smiled. "Whose eyes see all?" he said, quite positive that Ramon had sent the newsletter.

Chapter 11

It was still dark when Brian stepped aboard the Columbo Saturday morning. He listened to the creaks and groans of the boats moving in their slips. The sounds carried off across the harbor. He unlocked and opened the hatch and went below. Welcome coffee was found in the galley, and he put some water on to boil.

Some mist blew down through the hatch. Brian closed it part way. He reached over into the navigation center and switched on the exterior lights, fore and aft, and atop the mast. He flicked on the radio, and the maritime weatherman was reemphasizing the storm warnings and the hard weather front approaching that the TV weatherman had spoken of the night before.

Karen had co-anchored the news last night. It was a huge step, and he was thrilled for her. But she had a meeting today, and he barely had time to say, "Hello, good night, good morning, and goodbye," since talking to her that guilt-ridden Wednesday morning about this trip. Jessica was already becoming a little agitated and more demanding about establishing a time for their next "talk." And yesterday Brian had received the letter of warning Whipcracker had threatened him with on Wednesday.

The Whip had added "disruptive behavior" to "frequent tardiness," and when Brian said he didn't think the letter could be worded the way it was, Whipcracker had screamed, "Just sign the goddamn thing!"

"No one is more disruptive than you, Whipcracker. Where's your letter?"

"You said you would sign this!"

"I changed my mind. You sign the goddamn thing," Brian said. "I'm not putting my signature on someone else's piece of fiction."

Whipcracker grabbed the letter off the desk where Brian had thrown it and wrote, "Employee refuses to sign. Joseph Whipcracker." He added the date, and Brian walked out without being told to.

No, a little fucking storm was not going to keep him from the ocean this weekend.

Brian poured some coffee. The burner warmed the cabin, and he pulled off his jacket. Earnie would be here sometime soon. Brian was anxious to head out. He sat at the navigator's station and opened the copy of the Friday Blade-Tribune he'd brought along with him. The headlines in the second section concerned his post office. Pat Divers had come through. Almost three full pages were devoted to the troubles and mismanagement of people at the Bay City Post Office, and the issue of Injun Joe's was featured as the employee's only hopeful defense against the aggressive injustices served as a regular part of their working diet.

Acting as a complete and fair-minded reporter, Pat had attempted to gain interviews from certain managers. He reported their responses:

Postmaster Henry Whynaught—"If there's a problem, I'll definitely look into it."

"You're not aware that there is a problem, sir?"

"Er, I'll have to get back to you on that."

Supervisor of Postal Operations Phyllis Dunn—"Postal policy does not allow public access to internal problems."

"But there are problems?"

"Postal policy does not..."

Supervisor Joseph Whipcracker—(invectives deleted) "_____!"

Supervisor Lenny "The Weasel" Nicks—"No one calls me Weasel."

Supervisor Darrel Diamond—""You're from the Blade? Sorry, you have the wrong number." click."

Brian laughed out loud. He didn't know how much good it would do, but it did hold up as a very good article that accurately reflected the picture of activity and personalities at work.

One particular in-depth story caught his eye. He was much surprised to see the detail of the account that had been printed about the former employee Sue Brooks. Anonymous sources described how just four years ago she had been hounded so badly by Whipcracker that a meeting had finally been called to investigate the Whip's behavior toward her. The report said that Sue's husband, furious to find out about Whipcracker's indecent advances on his wife, had insisted on having it. The meeting was quickly set up and it included Sue, her husband, Whipcracker, Dunn, Diamond and Leonard the Weasel Nicks and the Postmaster, along with Bill Rose. The postmaster just wanted the meeting over, and Phyllis and her supervisors were a stone wall of exaggerated disbelief in the accusations. The informant recalled how badly the meeting had gone, with Sue, nervous and overwhelmed and worried about keeping her job, finally declaring that things weren't all that bad. When her husband stormed out, it was to beeline for home to pack. In his mind Sue had made her choice. Nothing she said in her defense could dissuade him from leaving.

Then things got even worse for her as Whipcracker turned up his aggressive advances. When his reportedly obsessive crush on her continued to be denied nasty things suddenly began happening to her: she was receiving late night phone calls; obscene notes were occasionally stuck inside her screen door for her to see when she went in or out. The reporter or reporters of her last days in the post office expressed empathetically how Sue was having trouble holding it all together as her fragile personality took hit after hit. And as terrible as these sneaky occurrences were in invading the sanctity of her home, things got persistently worse at work. At first she pushed back carefully, almost gently, still concerned about getting past her ninety day probationary period. But when Whipcracker's attentions got more and more inappropriate and aggressive, she finally told him off, and it developed into a big scene.

Brian sipped at his coffee, and shook his head. He had just started work in the post office, and he recalled wondering what he had gotten himself into as he watched the big fight on the workroom floor. And now he was learning for the first time all that led up to it.

He read on, sad for Sue and yet still very curious at the same time to know what person or persons had put together all of these details on this important segment for Pat Divers. Maybe Tom and Ramon...? He glanced back a few paragraphs. Bill was the only one of them in that meeting Sue's husband had demanded! This was a collaborative effort.

Brian nodded slowly and went back to where he'd left off in the paper...

On that defining day Whipcracker had crowded into her flat-throwing case, as he had frequently done in the past—as always ultimately invading her space, intimidating her—and he had started talking in the improper ways he had been talking to her on other occasions, causing great discomfort not only to Sue, but to any other clerk close enough to hear his inappropriate language. But when he tried touching her she suddenly and dramatically snapped, screaming at him and physically pushing him away. She had lost control, but he wasn't backing down. The fight was loud, emotional and long, and it was almost as if Whipcracker didn't care about anyone else in the office as he once again tried to grab her and make her listen to him. The surrounding clerks, at their cases or in the swing room, were getting more and more upset, even adding their loud voices to the battle, yelling at them to stop. Tom Short finally had enough, screw the risk of discipline, and he stepped over from an adjoining throwing case to plant himself between the two combatants, essentially forcing Whipcracker out of the crowded case. He flat out ordered Whipcracker to stay away from her, warning him that he should never, ever come near her again. If he did, Tom said, he would do more than just tell Whipcracker's wife about his perverted obsession with the young new girl at work. Whipcracker finally realized the attention he was calling upon himself, and he was reportedly very frightened by Tom's threats. He retreated into the offices.

But moments later he came out with Phyllis Dunn and Lenny Nicks, who allegedly witnessed the violent threats, and they removed Tom from the workroom floor, soon suspending him for the first time. Sue had only two more days to pass probation—two days—but she was summarily relieved of her job. No reason was necessary, since she was still probationary. By then it almost didn't matter though; she was already falling apart before the workroom confrontation finished the job. A few nights later her tires were mysteriously slashed and a brick was thrown through her front window. The next evening her separated husband happened to come back to their home to pick up a few things, and it was just in time to save her from her suicide attempt. She had sliced her wrists and had sunk into a bathtub of bloody water. She was in a coma for six weeks. Though he saved her with his call to the police, she was never the same again.

And life went on at the Bay City Post Office as if none of this had ever happened.

Brian frowned and slowly shook his head deeply angered by the revealing news. "Glad everything's back to normal."

At the end of the article, Pat Divers commented that this particular piece was referenced to unnamed sources only because of the litigious nature of its contents, and that he was continuing to follow up on the facts to support the allegations of the egregious acts reported in it.

The "Bay City Post Office; Part II—Sunday" at the end of the piece would read much like a threat to Bay City Post Office management, and after reading about Sue, Brian was very pleased to see how disturbing and uncomfortable their wait for that issue would be.

Throughout the rest of the report the manager's names were used as often as were quotes from Tom Short and surprisingly, quotes from Bill Rose about facts involving Tom and the managers. Bill had qualified his statements by saying, "These are personal observations that have come to me in my position as the local union president. They are not meant in any way to attack or demean the framework of the postal service as a whole, but to point out some correctable problems that have been created by a few isolated individuals who are acting, in my opinion, outside of their capacities as managers of the people assigned to them in the post office here in Bay City."

What could I get from a few identified statements in the paper? Brian thought. Another letter of warning? Bill had guts. He made up his mind and headed toward the lockers where a pay phone hung on the outside wall. The wind and heavy mist penetrated his sweater. He quickly left his message at the Blade for Pat Divers.

He got back and saw Earnie sauntering down the dock carrying a sea bag over his shoulder.

"Yo, mate!" Earnie hollered. "What a night!"

Brian was happy to see him, not sure until now that he was intending to show up at all. Especially after the night he had previously planned.

"Are you cured?" Brian asked.

Earnie threw him his heavy sea bag that clinked mysteriously, and he stepped aboard.

"Most awe-inspiring freelance sex-therapist I have ever had the pleasure of being treated by in my sheltered life! Yes, by god, I'm a heterosexual man again! I love women!"

"How many freelance sex-therapists have you been treated by in your sheltered life?"

He smiled and clapped Brian on the shoulder. "More on that later. Let's stash the loot, and, if the sea will have us, let's head out."

They went below. Earnie opened his bag on the quarter berth that stuck back under the cockpit. He pulled out a change of clothes, four six-packs of St. Pauli Girl and eight bottles of Mercier champagne.

"I hope you brought some food, Brian."

Fifteen minutes later they pulled out of their slip and motored through the harbor. They drank directly from separate bottles of Mercier as the boat rocked, even in the harbor. The maritime report was repeating the danger of the storm to all craft by one of the strongest weather fronts of the season. It would be peaking later that afternoon.

"Think it'll be safe?"

"I don't know," said Brian. "It'll be rough, though, that I know." They steered toward the mouth of the harbor and stared at the huge swells crashing on the breakers on both sides, rolling into the harbor.

"Damn!" said Brian. "I've got to go out, and that's what I'm going to do, even if only until this afternoon. I've got too much shit to work out in my head." He looked at Earnie. "Let me take you back in."

Earnie stared at Brian and said, "You must know me better than that by now." He climbed unfamiliarly, but with athletic balance, up to the mast as the swells viciously rocked the boat. He grasped the standing rigging and shouted at Brian, "'Your ancient mother, the sea, is waiting there—to put together what we are and what we can be!' I'll not miss that! No sir, mate! I'll not miss that!"

Brian laughed into the wind.

"You sound just like Charlie!" He lifted high his bottle of Mercier and shouted, "To life from the mother sea!"

When they cleared the dangers of the harbor mouth, they set the mainsail and cut the engine. For practice, Brian talked Earnie through a setting of the jib sail. They made a southwesterly course with the wind blowing over the starboard bow on a close reach. Some of the swells were splashing over the bow. Brian ducked below and came out with some of Donnie Bonito's yellow oilskins, and he tossed a pair to Earnie. The wind gauge was showing fifteen knots, and the rain began a slow but steady rat-a-tatting on the ocean.

"Bumpy ride," said Brian. "But not bad yet."

"Not bad?" Earnie gazed over the dark gray water with the many splashes of white forming on the caps blowing toward them. He said in admiration, "What a powerful motherfucker." He had a hand on the wheel and kept them accurately on their course.

"Now, that's respect," Brian said grinning. It made him feel good inside knowing that Earnie shared his feelings of awe for the ocean. He adjusted the sails for the best response from the wind then settled back on the cushions in the cockpit.

"Now what kind of shit is it that you've got to work out in your head?" asked Earnie.

Brian took a deep breath and said, "Work, women, home life; extramarital sex."

"Let's start with extramarital sex." Earnie said, "Jessica, right?"

"How did you know?"

"Duh huh," he said with as goofy a look as he could muster. "I saw you two during the crisis at work this week. Earnie's not as dumb as he looks, my good man."

"Couldn't be," Brian grinned as he leaned forward to tighten a sheet. "It's not something I'd want spread around." When he sat back he said, "It was the first time I've ever strayed since Karen and I were married."

"My lips are sealed," said Earnie. "It's one of those almost inevitable things that occur in a situation like yours. The wife loves her job; doesn't always leave enough time for her man. Her man needs an outlet for his work related anxieties, and has another beautiful woman constantly shadowing him with open sexual interest."

Earnie raised his hand to stop Brian's interruption. "No, no. It happens all the time. Man has time on his hands; opportunity, among other things, arises, and he rushes blindly into the inferno. Feels great. At first. But soon guilt starts gnawing at him, at his mostly puritanical soul. And worse, biological law takes over—the wife knows subconsciously that the affair has taken place. She doesn't even know why she is doing it, but she becomes extra nice, apologetic, more sensual. All adding fuel to the fire of a poor man's guilt. It's the law. The Biological Law."

Brian just stared at him. Earnie tipped his bottle of champagne, set it down and smiled.

"That's it, isn't it?"

"How the fuck do you do it, Earnie?"

"It's a gift. But I have one question. How was she?"

They laughed loudly into the now drizzling, low hanging sky, and for the moment Brian felt free of the emotional weight he had carried since his liaison with Jessica. It had been something that he had felt good and bad about, just as Earnie had said, and now Earnie had somehow made him feel that he could live with the good feelings without driving himself crazy with the conscience chewing guilt of the bad until some real decisions were made.

He turned the boat closer into the wind. The ride was even rougher, but the later trip back to the harbor would be made easier. Their course was nearly west now.

Earnie dragged a few pieces of Brian's rendezvous with Jessica out of him before finally saying, "This is no fun. Whoever heard of a sailor who wouldn't brag?" He proceeded to relate in salty language his own adventure of the night before. Brian laughed at the gay banter he had adopted and the educational tone of Samantha. And he was properly awed by the gymnastics that Earnie described.

"We were sitting back on our hands on all the sheets and blankets on the floor that had been thrown around the bedroom, both of us sweating and breathing heavily from our workout, and she was smiling at me. I asked her, 'What's up?' She said, 'I was just thinking that in a few more lessons I can turn you loose on the women of the world, but I may try keeping you for myself.' She said I was a good student."

Brian laughed. He said, "A few more lessons, huh?"

"Next one, Tuesday night," Earnie said while grinning. "Samantha said our sexual energy levels should be peaking again by then. I said, 'How about Sunday?' She said, 'We shouldn't push it. This is serious business.' I told her she was a fine teacher and that I would be on time for my next lesson."

"It sounds to me like she enjoys the teaching as much as you do the learning."

"God, she's beautiful and uninhibited, Brian. Maybe I can tell her that you're my boyfriend and she'll save you."

"I think I have enough problems," said Brian. He smiled and looked across the bow. "But I'll keep her in mind."

Earnie laughed just as the boat pitched violently through a trough. They were further drenched by the wave they rammed, and Brian struggled to pull them toward the wind. The steady drizzle had turned into a driving rain, and visibility was down to a few dozen feet. While Earnie steered, Brian reefed the mainsail to cut down on the wind it was taking in. When he had finished, Brian swung them back toward the southwest.

"Maybe we should take it back in."

"It's gotten too rough suddenly," said Brian. "We'd better ride it out. We'll be all right. Why don't you grab another bottle of champagne?"

Earnie opened the hatch and staggered below. With difficulty he handed up a bottle to Brian.

"Hey, what's this?" he shouted holding up the folded Blade for a second, then pulling it out of the rain that blew in. "It's about us!"

"You didn't see that yesterday? Check it out." Brian reached his hand out and pulled shut the fiberglass cover of the hatch while Earnie sat and read Pat Divers article.

Brian leaned back, absorbing the familiar and peaceful saturation of tranquility as it washed over him. Even in these cold, stormy waters, he found that quieting feeling that had always made time stand still for him, that time when nothing else mattered, none of the before, and no worries about the after. All that mattered was the now, the calm, reflecting, unmoving now.

"That cocksucker!" Brian heard Earnie's muffled yell, and as he wiped rain from his face he knew Earnie was reading about Sue and Whipcracker.

The wind continued to blow icy slivers of rain on its wing, and soon it penetrated the openings of his oilskin chilling him to the bone. The temperature had dropped fifteen degrees since they had started out. Brian locked the self-steering into place, and, after hesitating to see that it worked steady against the stiffest waves, he went below.

"Gad! Who's driving?" Earnie yelled, dropping the paper.

"We're on automatic, and...," Brian glanced at the monitor above the nav-center, "...and the radar's hot." Turning, he saw the tension in Earnie's eyes and he went on, "Donnie bought a state-of-the-art complex self-steering vane and servo rudder. We'll be all right, although I don't think we should leave it for too long in this weather. Besides," he added, "We can see more on the radar from down here than we can up there right now."

Earnie seemed satisfied with that, and he went back to his intense reading. Brian bounced against the stove and braced himself there to pull off his oilskins. "I've got to get out of these wet clothes." He stripped down and threw on some dry jeans and two sweaters, then wiped the inside of the oilskins with a dish towel from the galley before throwing them back on. "It's getting cold."

Earnie asked, "What's Tom going to do?"

"I don't know." Brian was rummaging through the cupboards in the galley. "Aha!" He pulled a joint of marijuana out of a small tin and held it up. "Storm relief!"

"Light that sucker."

Brian complied and passed it to Earnie who took a deep satisfying pull.

"Ah, yes," Brian said, exhaling smoke. "Good old Donnie Bonito. This is the least he can do after taking up so much of my wife's time."

"She's a good woman," said Earnie. "Don't blame her for trying to do better. And she is damn good on TV. From what I've seen of her, I know she's in love with you. Very much. The only difference between you two is that she loves her job and you don't love yours."

"Fucking A. You're right. And what pisses me off is my job can be better." Brian shook his head then grabbed his bottle from the steps where he had wedged it coming below. He tilted it up and took a big drink. He was getting drunk from the champagne and the smoke. "If Tom Short had his way, he'd shoot those sum bitches and solve everyone's problems."

"Everyone's but his own you mean."

"But he's out already. He's so pissed off at Whipcracker and all the rest that I think he might really do it. It's scary, but I almost hope he does."

"Why? Will it make any difference? Sure, for a while the sympathy and promises will pour in, but in the end it will all settle back to what it was, like ripples on a pond. Just leaving more scars for the terrible experience."

Brian shook his head slowly in disgust at the thought. "Bright outlook, Earnie."

"Well, it's the truth," he said. "Listen. Some things have got to change, sure. But do you think it will get better by agitating the shit out of each other? Someone's got to say, 'OK; no more bullshit from me—I'm sick of it. Carry on any way you like. I'm through fucking with you. I'm battle weary, and war sucks.'"

Brian took another hit. "Easy enough to say."

"Yeah, I know what you mean." Earnie took the joint. "It's like me trying to get over the Playboy Murderer while he's still out there. Some things are fucking impossible." He took a big hit on the joint and stared at Brian. "Let's forget about this crap for a while. Somehow it's OK to think about bad things out here on the water, but only long enough to realize that they're ashore and in a different world."

"It's just like you're looking down on them and can actually control some things."

"Yeah. Like how you're going to deal with them. But the bottom line is, if you can't change it or make it better—then fuck it. That's my philosophy." Earnie stood up when Brian opened the hatch. "But I still hope someone mangles the living shit out of the Playboy Murderer when they catch that miserable bastard. I'd do it in a heartbeat."

The wind slashed into their faces when they climbed out onto the cockpit deck. The boat continued to roll in the storm as the weather seemed to build up in intensity, and they bounced uncomfortably on the yellow vinyl cushions where they sat. Brian stretched out his arms to steady himself in the roll. He kept the automatic steering connected, admiring how well it withstood all the thrashing. He would report back to Donnie on that.

"I think I'm getting sick," Earnie shouted above the wind. The tossing about didn't help any.

"I'll try to steady us up," Brian shouted. "Close the hatch!"

Just then he saw Earnie's mouth drop open and his eyes go wide. He was looking past Brian, and when Brian turned, the monstrous wall of water crashed down upon them, rolling the boat over like a small toy, washing them into the sea.

Brian felt himself spinning and rolling out of control under water, battered about by the freak wave. He reached his hands out trying to grasp anything solid. He tried not to panic even when he realized he had lost his equilibrium. Which way was up? He flailed his arms for a few seconds, but couldn't determine whether his feet were above or below him.

The roaring wash finally passed. It had been a long thirty seconds, and his lungs were bursting. He drew on his last reserves of calm and forced some air slowly out. The bubbles tickled his nose and ears, and Brian turned and pushed himself in that direction. He kicked his feet and pulled hard with his arms. The sudden surface glow gave him strength. He shot out of the water to his waist while gobbling the air deep into his lungs. He bobbed back to the surface coughing and gasping.

Brian caught a ghostly shadow of the Columbo, a faded view that might have been his imagination it was so brief and unclear. It was momentarily silhouetted against the driving rain, looking like it had lost its mast, and listing severely from the water it must have taken on through the open hatch.

Brian had never seen a wave like that, even from northern storms venting their pounding strength against the shore in Bay City. And he'd seen waves at twenty feet, big enough to rip apart the Bay City Pier. This one had been a freakish monster.

He steadied himself with his arms. The water whipped at his squinting eyes while he tried to look between the rocking swells.

"Earnie!"

The hard sounds of the sea in the storm echoed back. He turned himself in a circle, and the panic he'd been holding off began to take grip.

"Earnie! Where are you? Where's the boat, goddamn it? Earnie!"

He spun part way around and stopped suddenly. It looked like a flash of yellow, the yellow of Donnie Bonito's yellow cockpit cushions. And there it was again.

Brian began a strong dog-paddle. In a minute he saw it again and stopped his stroke.

"Earnie!"

"Brian!"

"You son-of-a-bitch!" Brian swam hard to where Earnie hung over the long yellow cushion. Earnie was grinning. He reached his hand out and pulled Brian the remaining few inches. Blood was flowing from a wound on his head.

"What happened to you?"

"That fucking wave buried the boom in my forehead. Don't even know how I snagged this cushion. I thought you were dead."

"Here." Brian worked a wet tee-shirt rag from the oilskins deep pocket and helped Earnie tie it around his head. "We're alive!"

"It's so fucking cold."

"We'll be all right."

"And you thought I'd want to miss out on all of this? Hah!"

The wind still drove the rain hard, but the sky was getting lighter.

"Seen a boat, about, oh, so big?" asked Earnie.

"I think you've got all that's left of it in your arms. It was sailing out and down," Brian said. "Jesus, that wave was huge!"

"No shit!" said Earnie. "Now, where are we?"

Brian looked around and pointed to the right of the wind direction. "The shore is probably over there. About twelve or fifteen miles."

"Oh, you're just saying that to make me feel good."

They kicked their legs slowly in the direction Brian had selected. In the next two hours the worst of the storm blew itself out. The rain finally slowed down, but they still couldn't see the shore. The cold water battered them as it rose and fell irregularly, many times coming down over their heads.

"I can't feel my legs," said Earnie.

"I can't feel mine either. I don't remember ever being so cold. Let's talk about something else. You like to talk about women."

"OK." He paddled and thought for a moment. "You know, Brian, I don't think I have the respect for women that you have."

"You revere them. You'd like to strangle the Playboy Murderer because he kills them. You told me that there is always something good in every woman."

"But they're sex objects, a lustful outlet for my primeval urges. Where's the love? What the hell is love? You should know, you love Karen, I can tell. Even though you did backslide for the first gorgeous bimbo to come along."

Brian felt his face burning in the salty cold. "It was your idea, motherfucker! Remember your impassioned speech in the swing room? 'For Christ's sake, fuck her for mankind,' and all that bullshit?"

"Hey, no need to get pissed. But what makes you think I was so right? You think everyone balances their lives on my words? You've got to make up your own mind about some things. You've got a brain. I think you just wanted an excuse to fuck her."

"Well, I won't do it again." He kicked slowly then slammed the water with his arm before saying, "What I did was wrong. What if Karen decided she wanted to fuck some guy she thought was beautiful? I'll tell you Earnie; I'd hate it and deserve it."

"Only a few of us can go around bouncing from lover to lover. Some men can, some women can. But look at what we lose. You didn't answer me, Brian. Where's the love? Now, when I think about it, it scares me how I've been fucking up. There's a big emptiness in here," he said, tapping his chest before grabbing back onto the yellow cushion as another swell blew over them. "I've been a big game hunter stacking my trophies high, but not looking for the perfect mate—shit, not even an idea of what I'm shooting for."

"Hey, what about Marilee? You don't treat her like a one-nighter. Maybe you've got some feelings for her."

"Yeah," Earnie smiled. "That's a nice woman there. Don't let it get around," he said, "But I've got a lot of personal respect for her. And she's a damn good and understanding friend."

"That's it! She's a friend, not just a garage to park your car in."

"Yeah," said Earnie. "She is something special. If we ever get out of this ocean alive, I'm becoming a one-woman man. No more carousing, one night stands, large breasted and tight-pantsed bimbos. That's more than artistic respect, isn't it Brian? That's all I've got right now, isn't it? Artistic respect, one-dimensional objective respect. See an object, view and admire its surface beauty. Take it for my own pleasure. Time for me to find that one woman who will understand and grow older with me."

Brian laughed.

"What?"

"You, a one-woman man? Yeah—and we're here because I decided I wanted a mountainous wave to destroy a two hundred and fifty-thousand-dollar boat, toss me to the bottom of the ocean to see how much my lungs would take, and shoot me to the surface to lie on a cushion in icy water with a reformed libertine scoundrel whose bleeding wound might still attract some sharks to our predicament."

"Sharks?" Earnie pulled the tee-shirt tighter around the wound on his head.

"You're missing the point, goddamn it!"

"Point? Who cares about any stinking point if we get eaten by a shark?" He searched with wide eyes across the violent surface then tried to look into the mysterious depths below.

"Maybe I shouldn't have brought them up."

"Jesus, anything but sharks!"

"I'm sorry, Earnie. Let's say there aren't any sharks out here. Hell, if there were, they wouldn't attack anyway."

"Bullshit! I read the marquis for Jaws. I saw the movie. 'One by one they pulled us under throughout the night.'"

"You're making that up. That was a different movie."

"Yeah. The true one!"

"You've got salty ice water on the brain."

"We're going to die, aren't we, Brian?"

Brian stared at Earnie, and then looked toward where the shore should be.

"Of course, we are. But not today," he said. "And not in the jaws of some stupid fucking shark."

He started kicking his feet again although he felt it was an exercise in futility. He didn't know where he was at or where he was going. But now he was keeping an eye open for any fins breaking the surface. Damn that Earnie, anyway!

The sea began settling down when the wind began to slow. An hour later visibility had cleared to a point where they could see the horizon. The rain had stopped. The land stretched across the water in a thin line appearing impossibly out of reach. Brian's only consolation was that he had picked the right direction. But he had no idea whether or not they were gaining anything on the oceans currents in their drive toward shore.

Earnie had thrown up several times and was looking miserable. His teeth were constantly chattering, and he complained of a ferocious headache.

"Think we can make it?" he asked for the hundredth time.

"Of course! We've made it this far, haven't we? Be thankful. We could have been sailing to Hawaii."

"But I have so much wrong to right."

"Don't get religious on me."

"All I can think of are the bad things I've done. Especially to women. I'm no better than the Playboy Murderer."

"Oh, bullshit, for heaven's sake! Why don't you come off that Playboy Murderer jag?" He looked at Earnie, kicking the water and wallowing in his misery. His expression softened, and he said, "I've seen you in action, and I've never seen you show any disrespect for the women you've used for your own lustful purposes."

"Gee, thanks. Thanks a lot, Brian."

"C'mon, man! You know what I mean. The ones you go after are already thinking about the same thing you are and just contemplating your actions and playing their own games. I've never seen you force yourself intellectually or physically on any indecisive or troubled woman, and never on an impressionable girl at all. You, like Sterling Loudan? Is that what you really think? The Playboy Murderer? Absolute bullshit!" He kicked a little as he looked forlornly over the horizon. "That's all I'm saying."

"OK. This time I really mean it when I say thanks. It's just that sometimes I lose my cavalier spirit of virtue in the chase and question my good intentions in the end."

"Cavalier virtue...?"

Brian heard the whump-whump in the distance before Earnie did.

"Where's that coming from?" he asked. His eyes scanned the sky.

"What?"

"Listen!" The hollow sound was getting clearer, and Brian saw a speck in the sky. "There it is!" He began waving one arm at the distant helicopter. It was passing between them and the shore. "Over here, you son-of-a-bitch!"

Earnie's eyes were wide, and, weak as he was, he raised an arm. It seemed to be passing by, heading south, but turned suddenly and came toward them.

"They see us! Oh, Christ, we're saved!" Brian pounded Earnie on the back. "Hang in there. We're out of this fucking mess."

When it got closer, Brian saw it was a large coast guard chopper. In a few seconds it was kicking the water up, settling in above them.

"Karen!" She waved through the open passenger hatch. Brian helped the coast guardsmen who dropped down lift Earnie into the cage that pulled him aboard before struggling in himself to be pulled up. Karen hugged him and kissed his face all over. He felt like he'd just gone to heaven, though his jellied legs and weak, shivering body forced him to plop quickly into one of the fold down canvas-covered chairs. The helicopter roared and turned toward the San Diego shore. He looked back down at the yellow vinyl cushion rolling on the water.

"We should have brought that with us."

Karen laughed and hugged him again. She wrapped a blanket over his shoulders, and Brian saw that she was crying.

"I don't know what I'd have done if I'd lost you," she said.

"I love you, Karen." He kissed her and looked around at Earnie. His wound was being treated tenderly by a pretty woman in a coast guard uniform. Brian smiled and said to Karen, "Even out here he finds a woman."

Karen laughed. She said, "You feel so cold."

"I can't wait for you to warm me up." He looked at her curiously. "What made you come looking for us?"

"The storm had me scared and I was worried about you. After my meeting, Donnie started getting worried, too. He told me that he'd installed a phone two weeks ago that he had hidden aboard, to keep from Nigel for some reason. I didn't ask. I just got on the line and called. When I found out it was inoperable, I rang the coast guard and asked to speak to Captain Donovan."

"Your wife did a great report on our air to sea rescue of the crewmen of a Panamanian tuna boat last spring," the captain hollered back from his station. "I told her to come on down, and we'd go hunting."

"There was a phone on that boat?" Brian was stunned. "I didn't know that."

"It was supposed to be a secret. By the way, where is the boat?"

Brian thought he knew every inch of the Columbo, but he couldn't think of a single place where that lifesaving phone might have been hidden. Obviously the EPIRB, or Emergency Position Indicating Radio Beacon had not broken loose. Hell, maybe the boat still hadn't sunk. He decided to ask Donnie the next time he saw him about that phone. And thank him.

Brian told Karen about the gigantic freak wave and explained it again for the questioning coast guard officer when they landed in San Diego at the coast guard airstrip near Lindberg Field. For the next hour and a half, he and Earnie were routinely checked out by a doctor Karen had asked the captain to have waiting. He was looking for hypothermia and other effects of their ordeal. They were given sandwiches and tall glasses of milk which they gulped down.

Earnie's constant companion, at his insistence, was the pretty little coast guard petty officer who stayed with him through the statements and the doctor's temporary post where Earnie took several stitches in his forehead. He and Brian both refused to go to the hospital, and when they left the station they were met by some reporters with pens and pads and cameras and microphones. Rescue news traveled fast. All it took was someone picking it up on their shortwave.

Earnie was still accompanied by his petty officer, Beth Ann, who was retained according to his wishes for "observation"— although Brian didn't know who was observing who—and Earnie made it clear, despite her objections, that he felt Beth Ann had saved his life. Karen exercised a few learned moves in turning the reporters over to Captain Donovan, and they made their escape.

Earnie sought and received permission allowing Petty Officer Beth Ann to drive him home in her car, and Karen drove Brian home in their Rabbit. His motorcycle was still up in Bay City, and they would pick it up later.

"Donnie's going to kill me."

"He was more worried about you. I'll give him a call when I get home."

Night had crept up almost unnoticeably upon them about an hour ago. A drizzle began to turn into another hard rain as a new front worked its way south. Brian could feel as much as see out of the corner of his eye that Karen kept looking at him while she steered her way up I-5 toward Encinitas.

"You better keep your eyes on the road, honey," he said, placing a hand on her leg.

She looked ahead and started blinking away some tears.

"What's wrong?"

"I just don't want to lose you," she said. She wiped her eyes. "Not to the ocean, not to a motorcycle accident." She looked at him and said, "Not to another woman."

Brian turned his head and stared past the windshield wipers. A sudden emptiness gnawed at him. The rain pounded the canvas top of their car and he thought about how miserable life would be without Karen.

"I love you," he said. He thought about what Earnie had said and knew he was right. Karen wouldn't want him to tell her about what happened, just that he loved her. "And I never want to lose you, either."

"Let's find a way to spend more time together," she said. "I'll revise my stupid schedule." She shook her head. "Damn! I work hard so we can have more time and money, but I'm destroying the time we end up with now."

"You're almost there, honey. It's been hard on both of us, but we'll have that time soon enough. I've been thinking about myself and my own problems so much lately that I haven't given you enough credit for the difficult work that you're doing. You're the most beautiful woman in the world and the greatest wife a man could have. And you are my best friend."

He took a deep breath.

"If I hadn't been so concerned about my own job being so fucked-up, I wouldn't have lost sight of that."

He stared at her thinking about how badly he wanted to take her in his arms right then and there and hold her forever. "No, I'm not letting you get away from me. Sometimes I wish I were smarter than I am. But I do know a good thing when I've got it. I love you, Karen," he said again. "And I'll fight anybody or anything to keep you."

She put her hand on his and smiled through her tears. For the rest of the trip home, they walled themselves away as one from their own separate crazy worlds, and all the other inconsequential worlds around them, in the tender endearments that they had let built up inside themselves. Brian, after the traumas of the day and week, had never felt closer to Karen. Nothing mattered to him anymore except for the fear of losing her to his own ignorance and stupidity. She was under as much, if not more, pressure than he was. His work-related troubles were really trivial when compared to the necessity of holding on to her. Nothing could replace the importance of their relationship, their love. Nothing. She was everything to him. That night, as the rain came down, he took a silent vow never to stray from her or do anything to hurt her again.

Chapter 12

Everything exploded at ten o'clock Monday morning.

Ramon was the first to notice when Tom Short, in fatigues, stormed into the post office. Tom's eyes were glazed with furious determination, and Ramon didn't say a word to him as the giant man swept by.

The pounding of his black army boots caught Brian's attention while he was working in the cage. Whipcracker walked out of the hallway leading to the offices at that moment, and Brian was as horrified as Whipcracker when Tom reached beneath his field jacket and pulled out his automatic machine gun.

He shot off a loud burst at Whipcracker before he had the weapon under control and just when Whipcracker was ducking back into the hall.

"Damn it," he growled stepping catlike to the door.

"What the hell are you assholes doing now?" Weasel was running down between cases, attracted by the shots, and he suddenly looked like an owl when he spotted Tom aiming at him.

"You fucking killed her," Tom said.

"What?" It was clear that Weasel was shocked. "No..., no..., they told me to tell her...!"

He slammed against Marilee's letter case when Tom shot him, and he slid slowly to the floor. His eyes took back on their customary accusing look and fixed on Brian as if Brian had been the root of all his evils.

When Marilee finally let out the scream she'd been building up inside, only a few seconds had passed in the eternity since Tom had fired his first shots. Brian jerked his eyes away from Weasel's final hold, trying to understand what was going on—attempting to understand what Weasel was trying to say with his final words. He watched, dazed, as the others scrambled fearfully to the exits, nearly falling over each other, shouting and screaming as they went. He turned quickly and froze when he saw Tom staring at him.

"Go on, Brian. It's on me, now." He waved his weapon toward the back exit.

When Tom dove into the hall, and there were more shots and screams, Brian followed Tom's directive and raced outside after the others. Jessica gave him a quick hug of relief when he came around the corner of the parking lot to where a nervous group had assembled. It seemed like an unsafe place to be, but no one would venture out of the protection of the driveway to the street because they would be exposed to the front of the building, and that was where the shooting and commotion seemed to be taking place now.

"I told you that mutha-fucka was crazy." Jimmy's eyes were wide with fright. In anxious bursts, he and Ramon described to Bill Rose and several others what had happened. They'd been swept outside by the panic of the others and had missed Weasel's death.

"Macho bullshit," Anita de la Cruz whimpered. She held her fists to her face and was uncontrollably shaking. Marilee put an arm around her. "We have to get out of here!" Anita cried.

Several customers ran by the driveway opening toward the gymnasium next door. Earnie was flying by but hit the skids when he looked over and saw the unnerved group.

"Come on!" he said. "He's in the offices."

The offices were on the opposite side of the post office, but still adjacent to the customer service area in front. They acted on his command, though, and quickly followed while casting frightened glances backward when they turned down the street. They stopped in the parking lot on the other side of the neighboring gym, and Brian was breathing like he'd been in a marathon.

By the reports that were circulating from other witnesses, Brian gathered that Tom had finally killed Whipcracker up by the front door and the postmaster in his office. The timekeeper, who was the last one here to have seen him, said Tom had gone into Phyllis

Dunn's office and slammed the door shut. Apparently that's where he was right now because Bill Rose, who was peeking around the corner of the gym to eye the front entrance of the post office, hadn't seen him leave yet.

"What's he going to do now?" Brian's question was on everyone's mind in the parking lot.

He listened to the cars speeding along I-5. He welcomed their normal sounds to the sudden silence that had arrived. Soon, however, their soothing rumble was joined by the fast approaching howling of sirens in the distance, seeming to grow from every direction.

For the next twenty minutes, a second wave of pandemonium broke loose during the eerie and significant quiet from within the post office. Police cars and vans from Bay City, Carlsbad, Vista and San Diego began arriving and cordoning off King Street, Palm Avenue and the northbound off-ramp on the I-5 freeway running behind the post office and leading to Palm.

The people in the gymnasium parking lot were quickly transported by police vans out of the immediate danger area. A SWAT team had arrived and taken control of the many units in operation. They directed the local forces into safe and strategic positions.

The KMAA helicopter circled high overhead before landing in the bowling alley parking lot on the opposite side of the post office from the gymnasium. The bowling alley parking lot was larger, more protected, and still very close to the action. Brian was across the street in the K-Mart parking lot when the chopper came down. He jumped when he saw Karen assisted out by a member of the SWAT team who escorted her over to a SWAT van. He could barely contain his nervousness when explaining to the officer in the K-Mart parking lot that Karen was his wife and he needed to see her.

The officer spoke into a radio transmitter, and after a brief response he led Brian carefully across the street to the same SWAT van Karen had entered.

She was talking on a phone inside, and she looked up with a grim smile.

"Uh huh, uh huh. OK. Just a minute." She put a hand over the mouthpiece and said, "He still insists on me and the cameraman inside. He won't negotiate this, and he said for me to tell you that he's giving you ten minutes of no funny business to respond. He sounds very serious."

"It can't be done," said the SWAT officer.

"He says if you don't do it his way he will shoot Phyllis Dunn now and anyone who comes in later. He insists on making his public statement live, and everyone else will live." She paused uneasily and added, "He says I'm the only one he can trust to tell it to and guarantee that it's made public. I believe him."

"Damn!" said the officer.

"Forget it!" said Brian. "You said it—'It can't be done.' Not with my wife anyway."

"He's got us by the short hairs—'scuse me, ma'am."

"Brian, he's right. If I don't go in he's going to kill Phyllis."

"Better her than you."

"Brian, that's sick. He's already killed three others that we know of. We can save her life at least. And his. He trusts me. I'm frightened, but I know I'll be safe."

"I can't let you do it!"

The officer had been discussing it on his headset with apparent superiors and thinking it over. He talked to a communications man in the van who transferred the conversation to someone else while they waited. A response seemed to finally come in, and the officer looked up and said, "We'll set it up." He took the phone from Karen.

"No!" said Brian.

The officer looked at him as if seeing him for the first time. "You'll have to leave, sir," he said, covering the mouthpiece.

"You leave him right here!" Karen said. "I need him. Don't even think of sending him away or I won't do it!"

The officer sighed and said patiently, "OK, OK. But you'll have to cooperate with us on this, sir. We wouldn't let your wife go in, let alone anyone go in there, but apparently Mr. Short has a great deal of faith in her. We're all convinced. He's forced our hand with a fast approaching time limit and the fact is we know he will kill the Dunn lady if we don't act. We believe that if we do everything he insists on, he will give himself up without any more violence. We won't do anything from our standpoint to endanger Mrs. McGraw." He tapped his watch. "And he's not giving us any more time to think about it."

"Let me talk to him," said Brian. "I work with him, and he's my friend. He knows Karen through me."

"I don't think that's a good idea."

"Oh, for crying out loud," Karen said. "Give him the phone."

The officer hesitated, and then he handed Brian Karen's phone warning him, "Don't say anything that will agitate him. Remember, Short has a hostage. Her life may balance upon your words. Choose them carefully."

Brian nodded and took the phone.

"Tom, it's me, Brian McGraw."

"Ah, shit, Brian. Everything's in motion. Are they cooperating?"

"Everyone is."

"Yeah? God, I hate dragging Karen in. But who can I trust? I'm sorry, man."

"These guys are planning on letting you make your statement, so relax, Tom. But does it have to be Karen?" The officer tapped him on the shoulder and made calming signs with his hands. Brian realized his voice had wavered in his nervousness.

"After what I've been through?" Anger crept into Tom's voice. "Karen's going to be all right. I guarantee it on all that you believe in me. Who else can I trust? No goddamn one! That's who. You gotta believe me."

"OK, Tom, I..."

"Listen, Brian, I want to shoot this bitch, I really do. I told them that already, and they better believe me. You know I'll do it. She's the final link in the chain that fucked us over and out in life. And after I found out what they did this morning..." He suddenly growled, "If anyone looks over the top of those windows one more time, she's history."

Brian pictured the small, high level windows, the only windows to Phyllis Dunn's office, in his mind, and he could imagine the SWAT team trying to peek in. Brian turned to the SWAT officer listening in who had quickly picked up a walkie-talkie and whispered a hurried command to whoever was on the other end.

"What they did this morning?"

"Yeah, Brian. And now I want the world to know how these thieves steal lives. That's all. Hear me out and you will see why they are the murderers. Karen will be honest with me—if she says we're live on TV, I'll believe her—no one else, damn it. Only her."

"OK," said Brian. "But if you harm a single hair on her head..."

"No way, Brian! You and Earnie and me, we put the roof on the new church. We're all on the same team. It's nearly over."

"Just be careful, Tom. She's scared—we're all scared."

Tom took a deep breath. "If anything goes wrong, Phyllis the Bitch is the one I shoot."

Brian handed the phone back to the officer. He thought of how prophetic Karen had been when she had said she would be reporting this story one day. He hugged her while the final arrangements were being made. Donnie Bonito and his crew had arrived in the KMAA van, and the portable equipment was quickly set up for one of the cameramen.

After some frantic maneuvering, Karen and the cameraman were escorted to the front of the post office behind portable bullet shields held by two SWAT members. They stopped ten feet from the entrance where Whipcracker's body remained grotesquely bent through the doorway after some shouting by Tom inside for everyone to keep away from it. He was still keeping them at bay.

Karen and the cameraman stepped out and went through the other lobby door, while the two SWAT men retreated to the sidewalk. The officers remained armed behind their shields.

Brian left the SWAT van and shifted to Donnie's van where he could watch and listen to the proceedings inside on one of several screens. Donnie was in high gear setting up another shot from the front of the building and taping the walkthrough of the live camera on Karen's cameraman's shoulder.

"Wow!" Donnie exclaimed when the camera momentarily swung onto the violence of the postmaster's office as they passed.

Then Brian saw the look of fear on Phyllis Dunn's face. The barrel of Tom Short's automatic lay on her shoulder pointed at her neck. A small TV sat on a tall filing cabinet in front of the desk. Karen took over and Tom followed her suggestions while they set up in front of Phyllis's desk. He apologized to Karen and told her that she and her cameraman were safe. Brian was frightened for her, but proud of the way she was establishing control.

Brian was shocked by Karen's next request. But then he realized she was trying to present an easily acceptable ground rule while breaking up the frozen nerves they were both feeling.

"Do me a favor, Mr. Short, if you don't mind my asking. Can you keep it clean? Since we're going live."

"Of course, Karen. And you know I'm Tom. Just call me Tom." He looked at the cameraman. "And you can stop shaking. If you're with her, you're safe, too."

Karen took a deep breath and nodded.

"OK, let's roll it," she said. She told Tom to wait a moment while they set up the bulletin to go onto live TV. Donnie told her through their phone sets that the news was already dominating the networks, and that she was already on live. He gave a five countdown for Tom's benefit, and Brian watched as several other screens, showing the other live network shots, picked up in Phyllis Dunn's office. Karen followed, after Donnie's lead in.

"Donnie, I am sitting here under extremely tragic and bizarre circumstances with Tom Short, the postal employee who less than two hours ago shot and killed two supervisors and his postmaster, Henry Whynaught, of the Bay City Post Office." She glanced up at Tom as she said these words, and he only nodded.

"Karen, how is the assistant postmaster, Phyllis Dunn, holding up at this time?" The camera swung to her with a close up. Phyllis was an ice sculpture.

"Donnie, she is frightened, but appears unharmed at this time." As Tom motioned impatiently for the microphone, Karen held her hand up to him. "And I think Tom is ready to make his statement."

He smiled nervously at her and took the mike. He held the automatic up, pointed toward Phyllis, and said, "I know you got guys just outside the wall there. They need to settle down. Let me finish before you do anything stupid. Then nobody else gets hurt."

He glanced at the camera for a moment, and Karen said, "Go ahead, Tom."

"OK, thanks, Karen. First a little about what happened to me. When I began working here eight years ago, I thought that if I worked hard and did my job, I could be myself and go about living life my own way." He shook his head. "They said the same thing to Sweet Sue, when she started here. But they didn't even let her finish her ninety day probation."

He leaned into the camera and said more confidently, "Sue Brooks; remember that name, because I found out that they killed her this morning and, guess what? That's why we're all here now."

In the KMAA van, Brian turned wide-eyed to Donnie. Donnie made a questioning motion with his hands.

"It wouldn't have even made the news, but now it will," Tom was saying. "Oh, you can bet they'll say it was suicide, but it was murder."

"That's it!" Brian said. "What the Weasel was talking about!"

"What?" Donnie asked.

"Sue Brooks worked here years ago until Whipcracker started harassing her. They said she lost everything; her husband, her house...then she tried to commit suicide and barely failed. She ended up in the hospital in Encinitas." Brian looked at the monitor. "Now she's dead?"

Donnie's eyes narrowed, and he picked up a phone. "I read about her in that article," he said while dialing. "We were going to cover the story." He stared back at the monitor. "It would have made the news."

Tom was continuing.

"But these jerks," and he jabbed the gun toward a flinching Phyllis, "These jerks say 'No.' They don't like anyone being themselves. They don't want anyone to be happy or to have their own opinions or to have a good life of their own."

He jabbed the gun toward the door. "*They* can say no, but Whipcracker couldn't *take* no for an answer. Not from Sue; not from anybody."

"He was hitting on her," Brian nodded as he stared at the screen.

"Say again? Who on who?" Donnie asked, getting frustrated. He was now juggling two phones, using one to call his own information desk to find out more about Sue Brooks.

Brian turned to him. "Sweet Sue Brooks they called her. Whipcracker was all over her, and no one would help her out, not even my postmaster, Whynaught, when he had the chance."

Tom was droning on. "...they wanted everyone to be the same. Like robots. Automatons. Or ass-kissers. They didn't want strong people, they wanted people who would bow down to them. They wanted weak people. They didn't want someone like me. Everyone can't be the same, though. But none of us had anywhere to turn. No one cared about Sue, and no one cared about me.

"And I worked hard! Harder than anyone. But then they got together and decided to fire me! And when they found out I was seeing Sue, they decided to use her to do it. I've got proof of that, now. Ramon got a tape of Phyllis the Bitch, here, and the Weasel, and the Whip, and that chicken-shit bastard Diamond who got away..." Tom shook his head and ground his teeth. "Now they were pulling a fucking Sue on *me*. First her, and now me! Damn it! She was a good kid!"

"Mr. Short, please," Karen said softly. "You promised me you would try to be careful with the contents of your..."

"Yeah, sorry, Karen." He stared at her for a moment while he pulled himself together. He looked at Phyllis, adding, "And sorry Ramon." He shrugged and faced the camera again. "You see, we weren't supposed to let anyone hear the tape they made because Ramon got it illegally. That was too bad, because in it they made it clear on how they had decided to can my... me. It's the best we got on 'em. There is no proof of what they did to Sue."

He took two deep breaths.

"They worked like an evil gang. They said they would do it to me on that tape, and they did it. How? At first sight it seems like a lot of little things, I know; a lot of nothing. But eventually like Chinese water torture. It gets to you. So Whipcracker would give me shorter breaks than everyone else and if I put in for annual leave, they would lose my chit; anytime I said a word I was ordered into the office, and anytime he was setting me up, someone from that bunch would be peeking around a corner as a convenient witness to verify his lies. Even when they weren't there they became convenient witnesses! How could I prove any of that? None of the little things would have put me here, though. I would have stuck it out. Nothing until I read this."

Phyllis flinched when Tom rotated the rifle around to reach into a fatigue pocket. He pulled out a single sheet of paper. He stared at it for a moment.

"It's from Sweet Sue." He blinked his eyes and turned to the camera. "They told her I was dead," he said holding it out. "Weasel actually told her I was dead! He was sent there by that fucking Whipcracker to tell her I couldn't take my life or the job anymore; I was hopelessly despondent, so I killed myself. I guess they thought our distressed reactions to that would be funny."

He settled his hand on the desk and leaned sadly toward the paper. "Part of what she says here is she's coming to join me. And she... and she blames herself."

He sighed. "I tried to keep it from them, but they found out I was visiting her in the hospital over there. In doing so, they found the ammunition they needed to torture both of us. I was afraid of that...that it could happen, but I...I wasn't careful enough.

"She was amazing, people," he said, looking sadly into the camera. "One of the best things that ever happened to me. When I wrapped my arms around her, she knew she was safe. I think she was getting better. I'll never know now. I was all she had left after everyone else abandoned her, and they knew it. They knew it would drive me nuts to find out they were harassing her again; that they could still get to her. They were trying to hurt me, stir things up even more with me, but they ended up killing her. And in the end, my arms weren't there for her."

Donnie was holding a phone to his ear, talking, and listening to the action on the screen while writing rapidly on a messy notebook in his lap.

"Oh, my God," he said. "Just this morning? Yes. Got it."

"What?" asked Brian.

Donnie gestured in disbelief. "It's all true. She was found dead of a drug overdose this morning at the Santa Margarita Hospital where she was a permanent guest."

"...and where was Whynaught? We could have used him. But he had his head buried in his office and let these guys run all over us. This dishonest bitch, Phyllis, here, ran the show and the whole office while that postmaster coward said, 'Uh oh, uh huh,' and, 'I'm out of this,' in that order. I hate cowards. We were unprotected and always trying to fight back even though that son-of-a-bitch could have prevented all of this by taking a stand.

"Before this," he said waving Sue's note, "They had finally fabricated enough steps of discipline to fire me. Just like they wanted; just like they planned. Every lie they made up stayed in my records for the next time, and every word they wrote became gospel as my file got thicker and thicker. Who gets fired by the post office? Where else would I ever be able to work? Fired by the post office? Knowing that they could do something like that was, by itself, enough to drive a person to..." Tom glared at Phyllis, then he took a deep breath.

"Just like Sue, they killed me for being myself. They kicked us out of life. All we wanted to do was to work. What's wrong with that? Work and be ourselves. Have a normal life, you know? And who would be their next target?"

Tom was beginning to struggle putting into words what he wanted to say, and he shifted uncomfortably much to the consternation of Phyllis who was still looking down the barrel of his rifle.

Brian recognized the confusion as Tom searched for the words, the perfect words, words to express the things he knew about Sue's suicide in an attempt to justify what he had done, sure, but even words to describe his feelings about his last years in the post office; words that would not come, words that couldn't come.

He remembered the times he had tried to describe clearly to Charlie, Natalie and Karen the unjustifiable pressure, that overpowering atmosphere that made simply walking through the doors at work so frequently a Herculean effort; but the words were locked away—no believable way to put it—and he had been left repeatedly with the same loss of words that Tom was now suffering over, trying to paint a picture of the hostile environment created by the people Tom had attacked.

Nothing could ever justify what had happened here today, but Brian was struck with a sickening and confusing wave of understanding.

"You're doing fine, Tom," Karen said.

"Thanks, Karen. This isn't as easy as I thought."

"What happened here today?" she asked calmly.

He shrugged. "Well, I guess everyone'll say that I flipped out. Maybe I did." He shrugged thoughtfully. "I guess I did. Nothing to be done about that now. But don't cry too hard for those guys I killed. Believe me or ask the people who worked for them. Too bad you can't ask Sue. But she would agree with me; they're no great loss."

He thought for a moment. "Well, maybe she wouldn't. She really was sweet; sweeter than me!" He shook his head. "Actually, she'd probably be mad at me. Damn." He shrugged again. "Well, OK; I pity their families, sure. But I pitied their families before all of this happened, once I found out the kind of people their families had to put up with every day. Those poor souls didn't get days off like we did.

"But this morning? OK, I got up and visited Sue when I realized I wasn't going to work. When I found out what had happened to her it suddenly hit me, I finally realized that I wasn't going anywhere anymore; nowhere! And I knew why when I read her note. I knew why she died, and I knew why it was over for me, too. But just as suddenly I also knew what to do; that there was a grave error in humanity that existed right under my nose, and I came in here today to erase it. That's all. Maybe you can all learn something, now." He shuffled in his chair, looked at Karen, who smiled and gave a nod of encouragement, and then back at the camera.

"One more thing. The great and almighty union was no more help than our cowardly postmaster. The union officials who handled the third step grievances, the ones who are supposed to be soooo helpful, well, those self-serving pricks sold us all up the river. They said that when it came to our word against theirs," he shoved the barrel against Phyllis, who was positively cringing, "Their word was the gospel. Innocent until proven guilty? Fair representation? Day in court? Pretty phrases all in a row. Where's the democracy? Wasn't I an American anymore? Did that change just because I worked here?" He jammed a finger down hard enough onto the desk to cause some papers to slide off. "All of a sudden we had no rights?"

Tom turned to speak directly into the camera. "Well, civil disobedience and moral rebellion are partners in freedom." Then he smiled. "I didn't do it just for me."

Brian had the eerie feeling that Tom was smiling through the camera right at him.

Tom stood up, and when he saw himself go off the TV screen, he bent over to get his face back in the picture.

He shook his head slowly and seemed to be talking to himself when he added quietly, "Yeah, they killed Sue, and they killed me. I simply returned the favor for those soulless bastards. It's all on this tape," he said, holding up a cassette. "Listen to it. And gather what you will from Sue's note because that was the clincher for me. That's it."

He handed the microphone and tape and Sue's note to Karen and walked out of the picture.

"I...I think he's giving up, now, Donnie. He walked out of the office." The camera panned to a shot of Phyllis, who seemed immobilized and was now shaking at her desk.

Donnie asked, "Did he have the rifle with him?"

"Yes, he did. But tell them to be careful! I'm sure he's giving up."

"Quick! To the outside camera! And Karen, stay right there until they've got him. There's a line of fire out here you don't want to be in, just in case. Then bring me that tape and that letter!"

The live picture switched to a view of the windowed post office lobby. Two SWAT members were crouched behind portable metal screens, and Tom's huge profile was visible through the lobby windows coming to the door with the gun held over his head. Whipcracker's body still lay across the entrance, holding the door open.

When Tom reached the door, an officer shouted, "Throw down your weapon."

Tom stopped and then grinned down at Whipcracker's body. He still held the automatic high. But when he stepped over the body, he tripped, dropping his arms and the rifle down to catch his balance.

"Arrgh!"

In a horrifying fury, shots rang out from every nearby firing position.

Brian let out a yell and jumped up from his seat in the KMAA news van. He pushed the door open and sprinted across the bowling alley parking lot toward the post office.

"Karen McGraw is my wife!" he yelled at the bewildered officer who tried to stop him. The officer let him pass. Brian came to a halt after a few steps and watched two blue-outfitted SWAT officers leaning over Tom's body while another stood shouting orders. He finally saw Karen being led through the other lobby door along with Phyllis Dunn. Brian ran over and stopped suddenly when he saw that Karen was attempting to interview the non-responsive Phyllis until Phyllis was grabbed up by some SWAT members. Brian fell into step with the cameraman and watched and listened.

Karen pointed out to viewers the ambulance Phyllis was being put into, and then the activity surrounding the bodies of Tom Short and Joseph Whipcracker. They were all gently pushed back beyond the yellow-taped police barriers that were suddenly springing up all around. Despite his anxieties, Brian noticed and admired the confident and skillful authority with which Karen conducted her business. He understood why those around her respected her the way they did; the cameraman, Donnie, the police, and all the other news people. It was not only her looks and drive; it was her consummate professionalism. She was able to understand how the nature of her questions would be received before she asked them—what was most emotionally immediate—she knew what to ask; and she understood what people really wanted to know and the ways to get most delicately to the answers.

After a while Donnie gave Karen a message to wrap it up, that they were taking the live back to the studio, and she gave her cameraman a weary cut sign. Brian came closer and put his arms around her.

"God, I'm glad that's over," she said. "They shot Tom Short."

"They thought he was going to start shooting, But with all the shields and barricades, and with no one in his line of fire, it seems they could have waited to see what he was really doing. He tripped, Karen. That's all he did. And of all things, over the body of Whipcracker. The one person in the world who he hated more than anyone—can you believe the irony?"

They hugged as if nothing wrong had ever happened, and Brian liked the way it felt.

"Let's go see Donnie."

"You were wonderful." Brian kissed her. "I was scared for you."

Before they had taken half a dozen steps, they were surrounded by newspaper reporters and TV cameras from other networks.

"Why did Tom Short want you for that interview?"

"How do you know him?"

"What did it look like in there?"

Karen gave a weary shake of her head.

"You saw it," she said.

"Hey, you worked with him, didn't you? Was he always so violent?"

"Yes," said Brian. "But this is the first time we actually caught him killing a postmaster." He had a protective arm around Karen while he looked for an escape route.

"Oh, I know who you are! You were one of the guys picked up out of the ocean by the Coast Guard, weren't you?"

"Yeah, I guess I was a keeper." He looked around again, but they were cornered.

The questions kept raining down. Donnie Bonito finally worked his way through to them and held up his hands to the reporters. "Come on, boys and girls. Give these two a break. They've been through a lot. Let them unwind and they'll talk to you in just a bit. Thank you, all. Come on; come on."

He forced a path back through the cameras and reporters and led them to his van. He closed the door, shutting out the noisy activity surrounding them. Karen and Brian sat together on a settee used for comfort by the traveling crew, a crew who now sat at their work stations silently watching them. Donnie grabbed the note and tape from Karen, plopped down at a secured swivel-chair and began studying the note before looking up. He stared for only a second, and then he set the items down.

"You OK?" Donnie asked softly.

"I think so," said Karen. She looked at Brian who seemed more shaken than she was. "I'm all right, honey. I'm fine. I still can't believe it all, though."

"He wasn't going to shoot anyone else," Brian said. "He was right, you know; about all of it. They killed him when they killed Sue."

"Who killed her?" asked Donnie.

"Whipcracker, Phyllis, all of them, I guess. They were trying to ruin him. They couldn't leave him alone, could they? And they ended up killing her and now him. Just like he said."

"He killed three people..."

"They killed him, Donnie. Sorry; I still don't feel any pity for them. Not yet, anyway."

Karen put an arm around him.

"All right, I am sorry," Brian said. "But it's nuts! No one should have died, not even Tom. He was a gentle giant until they started climbing all over him. I saw it! You don't know what goes on in there." Donnie stood and put his hand on Brian's shoulder.

Donnie said. "Figuring out all of this will be the psychiatrists' and detectives' job, Brian, not yours. Remember—you are victims, too. Everyone involved is. This whole thing is crazy—bizarre— beyond anyone's control. You can't take responsibility for any more of it than I can."

He was trying to put a separation on it that even Brian could buy.

"Pull away from the inside so you can give it a good, hard look, OK?" He leaned close and said, "You might even be able to solve your own problems at work. But you've got to stand back from it all a little."

Brian rubbed a hand slowly across his face and sighed.

"Thanks, Donnie. But, you saw it! I'm still scared for Karen. She was right on top of everything."

"I told you I'm OK, sweetheart. My goodness, I wasn't as close to all of this as you have been!" She paused and then laughed at his look. "Except for that last part where I was locked in with Tom and that big gun for his statement, of course."

Donnie and Brian laughed then, too. It was a release of pent up emotions, starting slow and building until they all laughed hard together when the TV crewmen joined in. Brian mentioned how crazy they must sound outside of the van, and it made them laugh again until they were crying in each other's arms.

After a few minutes Brian wiped his eyes and remembered that he hadn't talked to Donnie about his boat yet.

"Maybe this isn't a good time," he said soberly. "But I'm so, so sorry about losing your boat in that storm Saturday."

Donnie dabbed a small towel at his eyes. "You know what a boat is, darling?" he said. "It's a hole you build in the water to pour your money into. I've decided that I hate sailing, so you've done me a favor. I was thinking of selling anyway. Don't worry about it; I'm not going to." He paused and said, "But my insurance company certainly is!" That started a softer round of laughter that tapered off quickly and uneasily. Then they all sat in silence.

A tap at the door was followed by a request for Brian to make a statement to the police. He followed an officer over to his squad car in the cordoned off area near the post office. A body was being removed by stretcher from the building while he answered questions, and he knew it was his last view ever of Lenny "the Weasel" Nicks.

From where he stood he saw Karen step outside the KMAA van to talk to a small group of reporters. Hunger and weariness were suddenly overcoming him. When the officer finished with his questions, he wound his way back to Karen. He slipped in closer and put an arm around her while politely answering their questions ranging from the murders to his ocean adventure, and he stoically put up with the mild jokes about making news for his wife to cover.

Inside the post office, the manager's offices had been marked off limits, yet there was still unavoidable work to be done in securing the mail. But no one seemed capable of or willing to take charge of the disrupted postal operations. It was after three o'clock and carriers were coming back in from their routes. They had left before the beginning of the morning tragedy and now they needed to get into the postal compound to park their vehicles and unload. They had all heard the news by now, and some had even come back early, before completing their deliveries. These carriers had been directed to a section of the K-Mart parking lot, but now they also needed to enter and unload.

Phyllis Dunn was obviously useless at this point as was Darrel Diamond, the one primary antagonist who had escaped Tom Short's targeted pursuit. Carrier Lou Lambier finally stepped forward to take over operations. He guided vehicles past police barriers to the back lot where they were unloaded and parked. The carriers were sent home.

Hardest hit emotionally over the entire tragic ordeal were the clerks who had been in the building during the attack, and especially those friends in Brian's group who had grown closer to each other over time by learning to get along with the others' eccentricities and temperaments. For the past three hours, most of them had remained next door in a meeting room in the bowling alley where they heard personal updates from some of the police officers filtering in and out around them protecting them from the press, and they watched the TV screens for the reports and updates dominating all the networks.

Earlier, the group had jabbered nervously and pointedly about the events as they ensued, but by now they were drained and withdrawn. Sandwiches and drinks kindly provided by the bowling alley restaurant were brought in to them, and remnants sat on the big table in the center of the room. Shortly after three o'clock they were released to reclaim their cars from the barricaded post office parking lot, and although many of them left, several clerks still sat sullenly around the table absorbed in their own reflections of the terrible events.

Outside of the bowling alley, reporters snagged clerks as they left in an effort to gain possible eyewitness accounts of the morning attack and edges on the story that other news people might have missed. They were met with varying degrees of cooperation and opinions. Several clerks expressed shock and horror and some lit up reporters' eyes by saying they knew it was coming. Jessica told them in no uncertain terms to get away from her as she tried to tearfully push past. Earnie walked up to an exceptionally persistent reporter with his cameraman who had cornered her and said he would shove the camera up his ass if he didn't back the fuck off her. The cameraman backed off.

Brian saw them and walked over with Karen. He asked Jessica if she was all right.

"Oh, Brian," she said while throwing her arms around his neck. "He's dead!"

He hugged her lightly and said, "I know; I know." A glance and he saw the uneasy look of disapproval in Karen's eyes. Gripping Jessica's arms, he said to her, "But it's over, now. All of it, Jessica. We've got to get on with our lives. I'm so, so sorry."

She wiped her face with her hands and thought about the finality of what he'd said. She glanced at Karen's frozen visage and looked back at him. She seemed to stare right through him, but he held her gaze until she resignedly yielded and pulled away.

"Are you all right?" he asked again.

"Yeah, great," she said. "This has been a wonderful day. Earnie, can you take me home?"

"Hell, yeah!" he said. He nodded at Brian and said with a shrug, "See you later."

Brian couldn't hide the burning he felt. She meant nothing to him, right? So why was he pissed?

"Excuse me, sir?"

He looked at Karen and was unable to read her expression although he knew that his emotions were unfortunately written in block letters all over his face.

"You've had a long day," she said evenly. "And I have, too. Let's go home."

Chapter 13

Thursday evening at seven-thirty, Brian parked his bike outside of the funeral parlor. He had arrived from work where things were still chaotic after three days. Several clerks were unable to face the scene of the tragedy and were on sick leave while awaiting voluntary transfers to other offices or undergoing intensive counseling. Their replacements and stand-ins for the missing supervisors, including Darrel Diamond, whose whereabouts were unknown to anyone except upper-level management, were unfamiliar with the operations. They served as anchors while the mail volume backed up.

SPO Phyllis Dunn couldn't bring herself to even consider entering the building again, and a transfer was being worked out for her upon her release from the Santa Margarita Hospital in Encinitas; ironically the same one Sue Brooks had spent her last four years in. A temporary postmaster was filling in for her and Henry Whynaught. His duties had thus far consisted of diplomatically responding to and controlling the bold actions of the wave of reporters who had descended upon the Bay City Post Office. But he was keeping his distance from the employees.

The clerks and carriers who had gone right back to work on Tuesday were still walking around like zombies, talking very little, performing their jobs in a perfunctory manner.

Brian moved down a quiet, dismal hallway. He stopped to look into a small silent room, empty except for a closed casket sitting lonely near the front. While he stared, a woman came up behind him.

"Did you know Sue," she asked quietly.

He jumped.

"Uh, no. Not really." He stepped to the side. "That's her, isn't it?"

She stepped to the doorway and looked into the room.

"I knew her well," she said sadly. "I watched over her for a number of years. She doesn't have anyone else. Not anymore." She looked in the room. "She was so sweet."

Brian saw the uniform under the jacket, and he knew she was Sue's nurse.

"I'm here to see someone else," he said.

She looked closer at Brian then, and her eyes grew misty. She nodded.

"He was her friend, too, you know," she said, almost defensively. "The only one who ever came to see her." She looked down the hall, then back into the room. "I thought he was nice... He... She loved him... And he..." She tried to blink back her tears. "I just don't get what happened to them." She was crying, and he started to reach for her, but she had turned and walked into the silent room. She drifted down to take a seat and he stood there feeling hollow. He watched her dab at her eyes and bow her head, and he struggled to finally pull himself away.

At the end of the hallway he came to heavy wooden doors that swung on brass hinges. He found himself entering a shadowy chamber. The room was dwarfed by the huge casket that was necessary to hold the large body of Tom Short. A narrow aisle was bordered by eighteen metal folding chairs with artificial leather backings arranged in three rows. This room, too, except for him was empty.

He moved forward to sit in the front row on a seat that was ice cold. The room was gloomy, the front of it lit only by the three tall candles that sat elevated behind the casket. The flames flickered dancing movements all around.

The casket was of maple and sat on a black velvet cloth that draped to the floor. It lay open to view. A spectacled elfin face reflected the green lining of the interior. Two wing-tipped bolts sat on the open door like disguised guards or angels preparing to lock the face forever into the deepest regions of a sad memory.

Brian saw at the foot of the casket a simple earthenware bowl. For a moment it didn't register—he couldn't believe what he was looking at. Then it came to him: Chief Leyua had responded to the death of his adopted son and was collecting the part of his spirit that had wandered into this cruel world.

Somewhere outside of the room a door was opened, and as shadowy movements reached a climax, one by one the candles blew out. For a moment all was dark. Slowly Brian's eyes adjusted and the dim outline of the top of the casket began to appear again. But now the stiff guardian bolts of blue steel were suddenly highlighted in the darkness, and an aura of smirking possessiveness surrounded them—like a halo.

Brian shuddered from a sudden and deep chill. He didn't pray much, but now he said a short prayer for Tom, asking for understanding. When he was satisfied, Brian left.

*****

The second and last issue of Injun Joe's showed up on Tuesday, a week and a day after the shootings. It was dedicated to the memory of Tom Short. The transcripts of the secret meeting were again included, and added this time was the transcript of his televised message. A tally of the events leading up to his suspension for the sake of dismissal from the postal service was provided by Ramon Lopez. Each event was supplied with the wording of management's file letters and followed in bold print by an elaboration on the actual facts provided by unidentified witnesses to the separate occurrences. The commemorative issue was sixteen pages long.

Brian had gotten together with Bill Rose, who had kept notes on all of Tom Short's discipline cases, and Ramon, who drew his facts with remarkable accuracy from memory, to quickly put together the issue. Brian ran the copy over to Charlie Sharp's house for printing over the weekend.

"Sure, I could do this for a friend," Charlie had said. "For someone I've seen only twice in the past month—I don't know."

"There has been a tiny bit of insanity and excitement during that time, Charlie. Geez, you know I would have loved to have sunk at sea with you aboard, but you're the pussy who couldn't make it."

"Pretty lame example. A true friend would have insisted that I give up my work on national security for one day of treading water in the Pacific Ocean."

"National security? Hasn't our self-importance grown?" said Brian with a grin.

They finished laying it out and making copies that afternoon, and Natalie and Karen joined them to finish off the address labeling over pizza and beer.

The newsletter was coveted with solemn reverence by the clerks and carriers and met with confusion and anger by the new managers. Copies had been sent to several major newspapers, and Injun Joe's final issue was printed in its entirety in the Blade-Tribune. Pat Divers had added heartfelt condolences to the families of the victims, and then supplemented his column with piercing editorial commentary summarizing the long-lasting effect that the old managers had made on the Bay City Post Office, expressing regret for the circumstances surrounding the long overdue changes and best wishes and hope for an improvement over the old.

*****

"This has got to stop," said the acting postmaster, Willie Peters. The short, stocky man with the salt-and-pepper marine haircut tapped a copy of the new Injun Joe's against his other hand. Most of the clerks whom Brian identified as his friends were over the worst of the shock of the massacre, and they stood defiantly listening to Willie's stand-up.

"Whoever printed this trash has made Short out to be some kind of martyr or hero. That's disgusting. He murdered three people!"

"Don't speak ill of the dead, man!" Jimmy said.

"Oh, Jimmy Winfield. You're the one covered with a veil of EEO protection. I've heard a lot about you, mister."

"Yeah? Well, I'd say you been listening to a damn select group of people up in yo lily white tower 'cause you don' know nothin' 'bout me!"

"Can't anyone walk in here with an open mind and find out things on their own?" Brian asked Ramon. "I can see how much better things have gotten already."

"Oh; oh, yes. Brian McGraw." Peters walked up to him and said in a lowered voice, "This is your wondrous work, isn't it?"

"We're all responsible," Jessica said angrily. "But not as responsible as you are."

Brian shot her a glance. "She's right, oh, Willie Peters. You see, whether you like it or not we consider you our equal. Always have. Sorry. You're just another employee like one of us. Being a manager you simply have too much power, and sometimes you abuse it as you please. You give yourself the freedom to ram home your own point of view with heavy handed actions while shutting everyone else's point of view out. However, whenever you or any other manager goes overboard in their zeal for discipline or in their delusion of superiority, we have a means of straightening out the facts and evening up the score now. We will never again be bullied by any self-serving vindictive managerial asshole who is abusing his position or be put in any danger by your attitudes. And the memory of Tom Short—whether you think of him as a good guy or a bad guy—will at least serve as a reminder to all of us to check you bastards in the beginning and never allow you to squash any of us down again. At least not in this office. That, oh, Willie Peters, is a fucking promise."

"He's speaking for me," said Bill Rose. "And I'm the union president." He smiled proudly and gave Brian the thumbs up. "Well said."

"And he's speaking for all of us," said Jessica. "Not that we can't speak for ourselves." She nodded at Brian and shrugged while the other clerks affirmed their support. "Now..."

"Well, now you..."

"I'm not finished!" Jessica said, and Peters looked stunned. "Now you can either stand here and jack your jaws and build your hate on the frustrations of failing to knock us down again, or you can go back into your office and do whatever you postmasters do—and I can imagine what that is—while we get back to doing some constructive labor for the public. After all, they are the ones who we work for. And despite you guys, we do a damn good job of it, too."

Peters face had reddened during the outburst, but he waited a moment after Jessica's tirade to see if any more angry words were forthcoming before he finally shrugged and shook his head. "A defiant bunch, aren't you?"

"I hope you can see what's going on here," said Bill. "Even though you won't be around for very long, maybe you can pass this on to your replacement along with whatever other one-sided observations you intend to add to the pool of bullshit you are compiling to describe our little group. Yeah, we're defiant. As you can see, we don't expect any more honesty from you than we have ever had from your predecessors. So we're not going to kiss your ass. We've been through a lot. Our skin is thick."

"Treat us like teammates, and we're there for you," said Brian.

"And we'll even let you be the captain," Jessica added.

Willie Peters held his hands up. "This is the kind of thing that trauma therapy is teaching you, huh?" He looked around at the half-lidded silence. "Nothing more to add?" he asked. "Then back to work, this talk is over." He started to turn toward the offices when Brian spoke.

"We want to communicate with you, Willie; but it's easy to see you won't listen. But, fuck it; what can you say to those who know everything?" Brian exaggerated his shrug and headed toward the cage amidst the smirks of his co-workers. Peters frowned and went back down the hallway to his office.

"Hey, Jessica," Brian whispered through the partition in her throwing case. "Thanks for speaking up for me."

"My pleasure," she said. "We've got to stick together against those bastards."

They looked at each other through the register cage screen, and Brian said, "I'm sorry for the way things turned out."

"Oh hell, Brian. I'm sorry I've been such a baby. You never promised me anything, and it was only one night. I guess I'm just pissed that we were so good and I can't have you whenever I want." She sighed. "I think Karen's a lucky woman." She continued throwing letters then stopped again. "I may not be so fast to say yes this time, but don't be afraid to ask if you decide you need another good talking to."

She winked at him and went back to work. Brian was smiling when he went up front to collect registers from the window.

"Hey, what went on in the stand-up?" Earnie asked. He was weighing up a package for the customer at his counter.

"Our acting-jack," Brian said, tossing a thumb toward the postmaster's office, "Is offended by Injun Joe's and the reverence it expresses for Tom Short."

"Uh oh. More of the same, huh?"

"I don't think so," Brian said shaking his head. "You would have loved it. Everyone's still sticking together, for one thing. And making a joke out of any of the irrelevant bitching that is so common from management, instead of letting the pettiness eat at them like it has in the past."

He was quiet while Earnie finished collecting payment from his customer. When he placed the package in the dispatch hamper, Brian added, "If anything is so important that it should eat at the gut, then let it eat at one of theirs. We can all take a lesson from you and Jimmy—you guys take everything so easily in stride."

"And Jimmy is protected by EEO," said Earnie.

"Funny, that's what Peters mentioned."

"And if we play it smart, we're protected by the threat of further publicity. That's what Injun Joe's has gotten us, if nothing else."

Brian thought about that while he went about collecting the registers. He was at Maxwell's register drawer—maybe he'd bid on Maxwell's tour when he retired next year—when he heard the loud angry voice at Earnie's counter.

"You Earnie?"

"What can I do for you?"

"You been fucking my girlfriend?"

Brian saw a young, powerful looking marine clenching his fists and scowling while leaning over the counter and trying to put his face into Earnie's.

"I don't know," said Earnie. He pulled out a little black notebook from his back pocket and thumbed it open. "OK, now what's her name?"

"Samantha, motherfucker!" he screamed.

"Hmm. Samantha Motherfucker," Earnie said calmly. "Can't find her." His finger stopped roaming the pages. "Unless she's the one with the special deep-throat technique?"

Brian was amazed when he heard the marine shout, "Yes, that's her!" He started toward them when the marine reached across the counter and grabbed Earnie.

But Earnie bellowed, "Cocksucker!" and suddenly bounded over the counter so fast that the marine fell flat over the rope divider behind him when he jumped defensively backwards.

"Earnie!"

Brian also swung over the counter and raced after Earnie who was sliding madly around the corner and out the door before running full speed toward the public parking lot between the post office and the bowling alley.

Just before he reached a yellow Camaro, Earnie took a flying leap through the air and tackled the man who was clutching a bag of fast food from the bowling alley cafeteria with one hand while attempting to scramble into his car. The crashing momentum pulled the driver out, and while burgers and fries flew from the ripped bag the driver landed hard on the pavement, and Earnie began pummeling him.

Brian was rushing over when he stopped, horrified, in his tracks. The driver was waving a gun, trying to line Earnie up to shoot him. Two shots finally went off in quick succession, and Earnie seemed to intensify his attack. He was like a madman who had met his match because the driver was massively muscled and had begun fighting back with every bit of the intensity that Earnie was showing. The difference was that the more and more familiar looking driver had that gun.

Brian moved over to the other side of the Camaro, keeping low, and totally aware of his vulnerability and the lack of rationality that put him there.

A fast approaching siren whined, and the gun went off again. Earnie screamed in pain, and there was a sickening, frightening thud. Brian didn't take the time to think about it—he dove with abandon over the hood of the Camaro and grabbed the driver who was on his knees lining up another shot at Earnie. Brian's momentum slammed Sterling Loudan, the Playboy Murderer, backwards, and the shot went off harmlessly in the air. Loudan's head smashed with a horrifying pop against a concrete parking bumper from the force of Brian's awkward dive. He tried to get up and he stared at Earnie.

"Who, who the fuck is he?" Loudan said before falling back to lie motionless while blood poured out of the back of his head and onto the asphalt of the parking lot.

His confused eyes stared back at Brian, and Brian watched while the life seeped slowly out of them.

Brian turned to look at Earnie who was sitting up against the Camaro's tire holding his left leg and grinning from ear to ear. His lip was bleeding from a deep cut, and his nose was beginning to swell up.

"Ha! I got him! 'Who the fuck is he?' Who the fuck are you?"

"Earnie, you're shot!"

He was still grinning. Brian ripped open the pant leg where the bullet had gone into his thigh. It was a small hole, and it had passed all the way through.

"Yeah, you got him," said Brian. He settled in a crouched position with his arms on his knees. A sudden calm swept through him. He smiled at Earnie and shook his head.

When the first police car arrived, people from the bowling alley and the post office had already surrounded Earnie and Brian, pointing and whispering. Two policemen got out and cautiously approached. One of them let out a low whistle after he had stooped down to check on Loudan.

"By god, it's the Playboy Murderer. And the fucker's dead."

"How did it happen?" the other one asked Brian.

"Earnie Franks happened," said Brian, standing up. He spoke loud enough for the people around them to hear. "He spotted this muscle-headed piece of crap, from the post office and knew right away that he was the murdering maniac who everyone is calling the Playboy Murderer. But Earnie went after him anyway, even when he saw the gun, and he kicked his fucking ass!"

A cheer went up, and more people kept gathering to find out what the commotion was about.

"Can you be more specific?"

"What's going on, officer?" asked Willie Peters.

"Who are you?" asked the policeman.

"Who the fuck is he?" said Earnie, still grinning from where he sat.

"I'm the postmaster, Willie Peters, and those two are my employees. They're supposed to be inside working."

He reached down for Earnie who scowled and said, "Who the fuck is he?"

"Earnie," asked Brian, "Are you all right?"

"Step back, mister," the policeman said to Peters. "These men just took down the most notorious murderer in America."

"Yeah, the Playboy Murderer! They done it, and I saw it!"

Brian was surprised to see that the speaker who prompted the new round of cheering was the same big marine who had grabbed Earnie over the counter a few minutes ago.

Peters backed off and said, "If there's anything I can do...these are two of my best people..."

"He needs help," Brian said to the officer.

"It's on the way."

The other policeman had been on the wire in the squad car. He hollered over, "The captain can't believe it!"

An ambulance wound its way through the parking lot with its lights flashing. Earnie was loaded carefully onto a stretcher while more police arrived on the scene. Their questions were met with the same euphoric grin and the same question, "Who the fuck is he?" Earnie was put into the ambulance. It drove away, with sirens blazing for its heroic load, amidst cheers and shouting. Brian laughed when he saw Earnie sit up and wave through the window. He was going to be all-right once he got over his private joke.

Brian answered as many questions as he could. He hadn't actually seen Earnie get shot, or a lot of the blows that had torn up the face of the Playboy Murderer, but he knew that Earnie was the real hero and made sure that the interviewers knew it.

He watched the policemen photographing the scene, the body and the car, and he saw the body lifted into another ambulance that drove silently away.

When the officer who had been questioning him told him he could leave, he walked through the crowd and back into the post office.

"You've got a phone call, Mr. Hero," said the new carrier supervisor, Lou Lambier, with a grin.

Brian walked past his fellow workers who had stopped what they were doing to watch in awe.

"All right," said Jimmy, finally.

He walked into the SPO's office and picked up the phone.

"Hello?"

"Hi, baby. How about an exclusive for an up and coming anchorwoman from the world's greatest newsmaker?" Brian grinned. "I'll roll back the sheets on this one if that's what it takes. Hell, I'll do it anyway."

"OK, honey," said Brian. "You're on."

July — Ten Months Later

The air was hot and the wind was light and steady in the cloudless sky. The sea gently undulated in blue-green swells. A pair of seagulls called out in harsh voices as they hovered above and behind the forty-nine-foot sailboat. The boat's mainsail and jib were up, but the pilot was making lazy use of the wind as he lolled in the cockpit.

Brian finished smoking a joint, and after discarding the remains into the ocean, he sipped at a bottle of water and placed it next to him on the cushion. His feet were up on the new blue vinyl cushions. His arms were splayed across the edges of the cockpit where he sat, and for a moment he stared at the automatic pilot that he had recently set. Out of habit he glanced at the above deck radar screen mounted under the dodger.

That day in late September was so much the opposite of today. So many things had changed since then. The atmosphere had been as heavy as his spirits, and the rain that poured down had drenched his soul. And that was the day he had lost the Columbo. He remembered, vividly, the ghost of the broken-masted, listing forty-nine foot sailboat disappearing like a vision into the sheets of pouring rain.

But that was also the day when his love for Karen took on a certainty he knew he would not again lose.

He leaned forward and tightened the jib sheet from where he sat before receding back into his reminiscing comfort. Donnie sure knew what he was doing when he had this boat rigged for single-handed sailing.

The Columbo hadn't sunk. It was found bobbing in the California Current about a hundred miles west of Guadalupe Island off the coast of Baja California by a Panamanian registered tuna boat. Donnie was less than thrilled with the discovery since he had finally come to the conclusion that he was no more of a sailor than his boyfriend Nigel. He had none the less pulled the Columbo out of the water at Kettner Marina in San Diego where Brian spent all of his spare time for the next four weeks repairing the damages and refurbishing it back to its former beauty. When the new mast went up, Donnie asked Brian if he'd like to buy it. Brian laughed until Donnie casually mentioned $25,000.

After Brian got over his shock, Donnie still had to convince him that he really didn't want the damn boat. That he'd rather spend his spare time partying in populous San Francisco or Tahoe than sailing the lonely confines of the sea. And besides, insurance for damages had covered most of the difference.

Brian locked his fingers behind his head and looked up at the top of the mast. It's mine, he thought. I finally got my boat, and wouldn't you know it—it's a beauty!

The money had suddenly been no problem. By then the reward money for the Playboy Murderer had poured in from all over the country. Evidently a lot of people had felt like Earnie did toward that piece of shit Sterling Loudan. A wealthy Texan had alone thrown $25,000 into the already enormous kitty after the deaths of the two UTEP women.

Karen negotiated only one point with Brian on the purchase of the boat, and on that she was adamant—he had to sell the motorcycle. "That would make a total of two fewer threats I could lose you to," she had tactfully mentioned. After all of his close calls—some she knew about, some she didn't—he made weak arguments for keeping it. And besides, the navy blue Toyota Land Cruiser he bought and used now to commute to work and to the boat was more practical, safer and more comfortable in all kinds of weather than the bike had ever been.

He couldn't contain the broad smile that spread across his face. He spent a lot of time aboard the newly christened Second Chance. As overworked as that name was, under the circumstances it couldn't fit anywhere else as much as it fit right here. When he wasn't at work or spending some mutually free time with Karen ashore, he was on the Second Chance. He and Karen often spent entire weekends aboard their boat, and this is where Earnie or Charlie usually contacted him on weekends, either by coming over or by calling on the celebrated phone Donnie had installed.

And Earnie—Earnie was in his glory. He was negotiating with an agent for the rights to their story and spending a lot of time up in L.A. and Hollywood, his old stomping grounds. When Brian had been approached by numerous publishers and producers, he told each of them that Earnie was his spokesperson. Brian grinned. He doubted that many of them had ever seen the likes of Earnie. Earnie, always ahead of himself, was insisting on playing his own role if the book actually became a movie, and Brian knew that no one could possibly play Earnie better than Earnie himself.

The Bay City Post Office had changed. After the confrontation in the parking lot with the Playboy Murderer, even the military-minded Willie Peters had relaxed his hostilities. Angelina Frohman was selected as the new postmaster replacing Peters whose tenure was only temporary while Angelina's permanent selection was being addressed. She was refreshingly communicative and understanding, and going to work had become a joy. She had incorporated the new E.I. or Employee Involvement program into the job, and, after some initial wariness, the clerks had finally endorsed it. Credit was finally being given for the hard, formerly unacknowledged work being done, and Angelina was listening to and acting upon the ideas for improvements that were frequently supplied by the employees.

The crowning achievement in their informal discussions, and the item that had drawn them into E.I. by showing them the good faith that Angelina was promising had been the installation of "I shall return!" Mark Adrienne "Teeth" Simpson as Phyllis Dunn's replacement as the new SPO. He *had* returned from Spring Valley, just as he said he would!

Brian scanned the horizon. In a few hours he would be in Bay City Harbor. He heard some bumping around below and knew that Karen was awakening. Her vacation week was up, and they had spent it alone sailing around Catalina, spending their nights in the harbors and dining in Avalon. Donnie found her too valuable to give her more than a week off at a time. Brian, however, had one more week to go on his extended vacation.

While Karen was going back to work as the number one evening news anchor at suddenly successful and top-of-the-ratings KMAA, Brian was picking up Earnie and Charlie for a weekend of "debauchery on the high seas," as Karen put it.

The clanging of some galley pans caused Brian to jump up.

"What are you doing, honey?" he hollered warily.

"I'm getting breakfast for us."

"Wait!" called Brian. He bumped his knee on the wheel in his haste. "I've got it, babe. I've got it! I'll make breakfast."

Karen smiled when he came below. She stood next to the stove with nothing on and casually dropped a tin plate into the sink. His eyes filled with the hunger he'd always had for her naked body.

Karen said, "I knew that would get you down here." She glanced up toward the cockpit. "Are we good?"

"I'm on autopilot, and the radar is hot!"

Some things never change.

####

Thank you for reading Post Office. If you enjoyed it, won't you please take a moment to leave me a review at your favorite retailer?

Thank you so much!

Tim Reaume

Discover other titles by Tim Reaume:

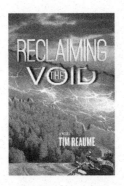 

Reclaiming The Void: After only a few glasses of wine the night before, Neil has no idea what happened next or how he ended up in his own bed in the morning. It's when he grabs his head in pain that he notices the blood on his tee-shirt. It's not his blood...

His life in peril, he tries to stay one step ahead of the police, as well as the victim's wealthy husband, Thomas Van der Worth, and a rival motorcycle gang, the Cula Crew. His personal investigation is bolstered by his own motorcycle club, as well as the unexpected assistance of an ancient, reclusive mobster and the welcome intervention of a resourceful woman who saves his life and then steals his heart.

The Jade Jaguar: A musician and college student from Saginaw Valley State University, Michael Dryden—Moon to all who know him—has dreamed of the Jade Jaguar his entire life, never understanding those dreams. But then, because of a chance encounter with a young Mayan, he learns of the true existence of that mystical idol.

Grabbing his motley crew of band mates, Moon heads into the bizarre and dangerous world of entangled lives and human sacrifices in the jungles and history rich world of the Maya. And suddenly, as Moon gets closer to his destination, more deep and deadly secrets of the Jade Jaguar begin coming to light.

Acknowledgments:

Special thanks to the many people who have encouraged me more than they will ever know: Dr. Raymond Tyner; Mrs. Glover and Mrs. Joy Wilson; and my pseudo-padre Ted Nitz. John Bowman is my mentor and friend, and just being around him to discuss the things we love is an amazing joy to me. There is no stronger influence in your life than from someone who will take the time to listen and understand, and then actually encourage your creativity even when what you have done is only a work in progress. Loving, discerning people like those I mentioned see that you are, too, a work in progress.

Many thanks to Mark Melchor, Tracy Bacholzky, Marc Sylwestrzak, Michel Sylwestrzak, for their encouraging words and support. Thanks also, to Stacey Cabral-Levesque and Robin Reaume Jones for their input on earlier drafts of my book. Thanks to Shane Reaume and Pat Reaume for their insightful comments, as well. A very special thanks to Amy Sylwestrzak at **Web Cabbage Creative** for the beautiful cover she designed for my book.

I want to thank Adrienne Deegan for allowing me to use her thirty six footer as my office while I outlined and developed the lion's share of the story of Post Office. Thank you, Adrienne, from the bottom of my heart for your generosity, and as well for sharing your fine sailing knowledge during the times we were able to hit the open waters of the Pacific together.

Many thanks to a very special friend, Craig Anderson, living in the land down under. Our long distant encouragements have moved us both along in very good ways, even from our worlds apart. You are an amazing and wonderful person, and I thank God for that most unusual encounter that somehow led to our friendship.

And finally, special thanks to Virginia Sylwestrzak for her endless inspiration and boundless love. It is not hyperbole to say I would be nothing without her. She was—and is—my mother and always my number one supporter, and I love her dearly and miss her much.

About the Author

I have spent time on both sides of the fence in the post office, working as a clerk, and working as a manager. Prior to that, I worked in an iron foundry, shoveling black sand, building molds, pouring iron, and shifting weights; served in the Army for three years; worked as a carpenter and wrote for several city newspapers. Nowadays when I am not immersed in a writing venture I stay busy and have just as much fun pounding out tunes on my guitar, competing in Texas Hold 'Em tournaments, or wandering around our little world with my lovely wife, simply taking in the diverse beauty of the magnificent realm of sky, land and sea surrounding us in our joyfully hectic home in Southern California.

CPSIA information can be obtained
at www.ICGtesting.com
Printed in the USA
BVOW03s0851201217
503308BV00007B/2336/P